Praise for *Orphans*

"In this brief, luminous text, a meditation on damage, loss and survival, the narrator, a latter-day Everyman, presents us with nothing less than a secret spiritual history of the post-war world—our world, in which we are all survivors."

— John Banville

"An extraordinary novel, full of rare and palpable feeling, reminiscent of Sebald or Thomas Mann."

— Frédéric Beigbeder

"His three novels … have placed Hadrien Laroche at the forefront of contemporary French writing."

— Sylvain Bourmaud, *Libération*

"Hadrien Laroche describes with masterful art the broken spirit of a lost generation."

— Marie-Claire Blais

ORPHANS

HADRIEN LAROCHE

Translated by Jan Steyn and Caite Dolan-Leach

DALKEY ARCHIVE PRESS
Champaign / London / Dublin

Originally published in French as *Les Orphelins* by Éditions Allia, Paris, 2005

Copyright © 2005 by Éditions Allia

Translation copyright © by Jan Steyn and Caitlin Dolan Leach

First edition, 2014

Library of Congress Cataloging-in-Publication Data

Laroche, Hadrien, 1963-
    [Orphelins. English]
    Orphans / Hadrien Laroche ; translated by Jan Steyn and Caite
    Dolan-Leach. -- First edition.

    pages cm
    ISBN 978-1-62897-002-9 (pbk. : alk. paper)

    1. Orphans--Fiction. 2. Psychic trauma--Fiction. 3. Grief--Fiction.
    I. Steyn, Jan H., translator. II. Dolan-Leach, Caite. III. Title.
    PQ2672.A6875O8613 2014
     843'.914--dc23

                        2014016359

Partially funded by the Illinois Arts Council, a state agency

www.dalkeyarchive.com

Cover: design and composition by Mikhail Iliatov
Printed on permanent/durable acid-free paper

ORPHANS

TRANSLATORS' NOTE

We've known since Plato that all texts are orphans, abandoned by parents who are no longer present to answer for them. A work in translation is orphaned twice. A reader's questions cannot be answered in advance, not by an author and certainly not by a translator, not without it becoming something other than a question. Yet we feel responsible for these unresponsive *Orphelins* turned *Orphans*, and feel compelled to say one or two things in their defense.

The first "untranslatable" with which readers are confronted is the title of the book itself. The French *orphelins* carries a slightly different meaning than the English *orphans*: in French, an orphan is someone who has lost one or both of their parents, while in English the title "orphan" is reserved for someone whose parents are both dead.

Appropriately for a book that is explicitly concerned with parentage and descent, "né" (masculine) or "née" (feminine) presented some difficulty. Literally meaning "born," indicating names given at birth, we have kept them in their French forms.

And finally, there is the tricky business of the author's name, variations of which have been inserted throughout this "parentless" text. "Hadrien" is another "H" name; indeed, in the original French, all the characters' first names were demarcated only by this initial (H. née Bloch, H. née Bouttetruie, etc.). His last name, Laroche, means "the rock" in French, and we've consistently used the word "rock" wherever it appears.

   – CDL & JS

HANNAH NEE BLOCH

HANNAH née Bloch was urinating standing upright in a hipbath, thinking of her mother. The stream from the showerhead came down over her voluptuous earthy body, dampening her crest of gray hair, running down the wrinkles on her face, flowing around her owl-like eyes, forming large gray discs around her hazel pupils, following the happy curves of her maternal and musky bosom, drenching her large, round belly and the fold of her navel, where she had been nourished by her now hundred-year-old mother, passing down to her dripping pubis where water mixed with urine, hardly changing color as it trickled over those considerable legs, down her thighs, and then her calves, where life only recently circulated between Scylla and Charybdis, among the itinerant blood clots in the purple-blue stream of her arteries.

That morning, she was once more reborn. She frolicked. The bathroom was similar to the stateroom containing an entire ship's crew in that Marx Brothers' film, or the one where Witold Gombrowicz, the author of *Pornografia*—a writer who, like herself, hails from Central Europe—spent a night upon leaving Poland for good: "And so I distance myself," he wrote. "Without ever returning. I distance myself and I don't know what is happening behind me." Beyond the shower, the room looked like the ark saved from shipwreck, as if devastation had been visited on the place by a sudden sea storm. The walls were splattered from floor to ceiling, small puddles forming in the bidet, the washbasin, and on the vintage 1960s yellow-and-blue tiling. She left the bathroom wrapped in a towel the size of a bedspread, its pattern a masterpiece painting depicting a battle, or perhaps even the size of a Bedouin tent under which a large clan—cousins, nephews, grandparents—an entire community could live, eat, and sleep. Underneath her cloth of gold, in reality a threadbare towel rough from regular washing, her body busied itself in the kitchen from early in the morning for virtually the whole day. Hannah née Bloch derived savory sustenance from chicken legs accompanied by cloves of garlic and horseradish. For the moment, she silently went into the kitchen, then left it having loaded her plate with breakfast. Knife in hand, facing me, she buttered her bread, daydreaming about her mother.

Having met her on the train, upon disembarking onto the platform, she unceremoniously offered to put me up. I was now staying at this woman's house for an indefinite period, hoping to catch my breath after years of living a difficult, exhausting, and gloomy life, which I had recently attempted to bring to an end. The bread she was slicing that morning was of a particular type. A few days after my arrival, she had found this type of bread, something between a "*bâtard*" and a "*flute*," being sold by an organic produce vendor—it was three times as thick as a baguette, and one and a half meters in length, produced partly for establishments serving hundreds of lunches to workers in backrooms filled with the cigarette smoke of perennial lottery players, but even more for those isolated farms that wait patiently year-round for the weekly bread delivery. As I saw her, she was transporting this bread in a caddy that seemed to have been acquired specifically for the purpose. Protected by a tartan canvas cloth, it stood there, upright. Only its head, round and cracked, and hard of crust, stuck out above the wheeled contraption. After her discovery of this abominable food product, not a week would go by without her coming home, armed with this horrible *bâtard*—a "bastard" bread—which would already become dry, even stale, after a single night. So much so that I can write that the *bâtard* and I arrived at and stayed in the home of Hannah née Bloch at more or less the same time: the *bâtard* came in the cart, I by way of the emergency stairway (the elevator was out of service on that first day). Such a loaf could never be appropriate for a two-person household, even one temporarily augmented by a visitor. This bread satisfied some purpose other than edibility. In its stale form, the object no doubt fulfilled some magic function for her. It exorcised her fear of hunger, the threat of a clash of civilizations and, beyond that, her childhood recollections of spending the war in hiding. Something further? Unsuitable for breakfast after two days in the house, Hannah transformed the *bâtard* in numerous ways: bread fingers for dipping into soft-boiled eggs, croutons for use in omelets and onion soup, and then, as a last resort, breadcrumbs. Crumbs packed and kept in Tupperware containers stacked in the mini-pantry underneath the table, which was covered with a checkered oilcloth. My relationship with the crumbs was just as visceral as with the bread. Whenever I had an opportunity, I tried to get rid of them, as if they were my own. And so the trash cupboard became an important ally. Soon enough, however, she relegated care of the *bâtard* to me. It was I who brought it home when she was not there, I who wrapped it in a rag, I who changed the diaper, so to speak. Finally, it was I who condemned the *bâtard* to sleeping in the little nook underneath the kitchen cupboard where I would tuck this cumbersome progeny into a large drawer, before sliding it all the way shut. That morning she sliced an entire baguette's worth of bread into little rounds about the size of a napkin ring engraved with the name of a son, something one would not find in her house. Wide-eyed and bushy-tailed at this early hour, facing a slab of fresh butter, an assortment of cheeses, milk, the coffee tin, or the vinegar jar, she now fried the crusty ends on a gas stove, still thinking about her mother. In the apartment decorated with natural furniture, made out of wood or rattan, there were some pieces that were salvaged and others that had been perverted from their normal use. The base of a Singer sewing machine—with black iron pedals—served as a kitchen table. The formerly ribbed backs of chairs were patched up with sheets of plywood, no doubt picked up off the street. A fresco covered an entire living-room wall on the thirteenth floor of this social housing project building. It depicted an enormous rooster. A colorful bird, its head topped with a red crest, its green eye full of terrible intensity, its presence dazzling.

Hannah née Bloch had difficulties with her hearing, fewer, however, than her twin brother—Henri né Bloch—who was also, as the expression goes, hard of hearing, to the point of deafness. My host—I say "host" because I suppose I was a sort of guest—had turned the volume dial on the belly of the telephone all the way up, jamming it to the highest level; an ear-piercing tone resounded with every call. On rare occasions, the telephone in the apartment would ring and there would always be some family member on the other end of the wireless handset: Hannah née Bloch's husband, twin brother, or hundred-year-old mother. The husband was a cabinetmaker. He rented a workshop in the neighborhood and would go there every morning. The workshop was closed for lunch, which he would eat at home, on the Singer table, and then open again through the afternoon until nighttime. He worked without cease. Endlessly bent over his workbench. When he got home at night, the intercom—also set to a volume that could wake a sleeping battalion—would carry the steady voice of a man who, without greeting or asking who was on the other end, would ask "D'YOU HAVE ANY BREAD?!" No doubt having failed to notice the *bâtard*. Early in the morning, while her husband prepared to leave, there were two voices equally likely to come crackling over the phone: her brother's and her mother's. This morning's call was from her brother. During all the time I spent living with Hannah née Bloch, I never saw an outsider enter the apartment or heard one speaking, other than myself that is. The mother and daughter spoke somewhere between three and a hundred times per day. I spent most of my time during this period in my temporary room, busying myself with idle projects. The ringing would wake me from my torpor and I would hear the conversation and would end up listening to the stream of commentary that would inevitably follow each call. By the end of the day, the threads of these numerous monologues would be woven into an immense canvas covering the entire house, like those white sheets one drapes over the furniture before leaving for a long time or after a death. Conversations with the mother would lead to conversations with the brother. He lived in a furnished apartment on the same corridor as the one his mother lived on; their respective rooms were separated only by a thin partition. Thin enough that the son would hear the conversations between his sister and the old lady. Nonetheless, when the twins were on the phone together they would keep recounting things that they had both already heard, either through the earpiece or through the wall. Later in the day, when she phoned her husband, Hannah née Bloch would repeat to him, not the conversation with her brother, nor the one with her mother, but rather the audible commentary I could hear her making to herself after hanging up. Riddled with words from assorted languages, cracks in her voice, and sudden exclamations, these telephonic soliloquies would, without exception, terminate in little cries of despair. Finally, after an argument with her mother, she would hang up the phone only to call back a few minutes later in order to apologize. It's hard to reconstruct the gist of these conversations from only the brief responses I heard behind the door. However, I had documents to aid me. By means of a little recording device that she held up against the upper part of the handset, which I saw her do many times, Hannah née Bloch effectively archived these conversations. 33 RPM audio cassette tapes, which she then tossed in a trunk in her bedroom, simply noting the name of her interlocutor and the date of the exchange on a sticky label. For lack of organization, they piled up. However, she had filed away a hundred or so of these tapes in a drawer of a writing desk that sat next to her bed. I calculated that they held two hundred and sixty hours of recordings, corresponding to two thousand seven hundred and ninety-two conversations, the length of which varied from fifteen seconds to an hour and a half. Printed out, these audio recordings would fill twenty one-hundred-page volumes, making for two thousand cramped pages. I was able to listen to several of these tapes while she was napping or when she went out. Although the majority contained all kinds of silences that were much longer than the snippets of sentences or the few words that separated these blank spots—forced silences, short sighs, hiccups, asides, whistles, throat-clearings, farts—they did nevertheless contain several memorable pieces. Two tapes bore additional red labels with the notation: diatribe. I discovered these belatedly. Also—based on samples of those numerous and daily telephonic soliloquies with her mother, heard from behind the door of my room, and from conversations with her husband in the kitchen over the Singer sewing machine (conversations which took place in my presence, at breakfast, at least the first few times), as well as from these bags filled with taped recordings I had stumbled across one day—I was able, in the chaos, to propose pieces of an explanation for the possible origins, or probable causes, of the dispute between Hannah née Bloch and her mother. If explanations were necessary.

The Bloch family had arrived from Central Europe towards the end of the twenties of the last century. The parents and their only daughter—born before the exile, not far from Zakopane—had settled in on the second floor of a modest building in the center of G. The father made a living by barter. He owned a shed on the banks of the Isère where he stocked various objects. Chandeliers, candlesticks, pelisses, he conducted his business in a cart pulled by a donkey, crying out beneath the windows of the city: *"Alte Sachen! Alte Sachen!"* which everyone heard as *"Akisakin,"* and which no one understood. The twins were born shortly after the young couple and their daughter arrived. It snowed on the day of the dead that year. Twelve years later, the father was among the first of those deported to Germany, via a concentration camp also situated on the bank of the Isère. Some months later, on a Thursday morning, a police patrol appeared at the family's residence; while everyone made themselves small and silent, the eldest daughter went to open the door and stated that there was no one in the apartment. The police looked in from the threshold of the modest dwelling: a bathtub in the kitchen, a table, a radiator on wheels, a mattress on the floor covered with down quilts. They didn't enter. They returned in an hour to takeaway the Jewish tenants, women and children alike. More than enough time for the mother to send each of her children to the house of a neighbor born to Catholic parents, to a cousin's house on the other side of the river, or to the back of a shop of an aunt who sold spices on the Avenue Alsace-Lorraine: cinnamon, cumin, vanilla, saffron. The mother also took to her heels. Half a century later, this scene—or the fantasy of it—kept coming up in the eternal conversation sustained between Hannah née Bloch and her mother or her brother. Ratiocinations sustained by the status and position of the eldest child: it was he—or, in this case, she—who was the designated primary recipient of whatever the parents unwittingly transmitted. According to the twins, by opening the door, the eldest daughter could have condemned the family to death. According to the mother, it was quite the opposite: it was precisely this gesture that had saved the family from fire and gas. By barring the way with her sickly, deformed body—a truly repulsive body I once found myself mashed up against in the elevator, hunchbacked and warped—she had blocked the policemen's access to the hearth. The twins' version relied on other facts and actions undertaken by the eldest child: for example, she wouldn't hesitate to parade down the street in front of the German soldiers, the Jewish star stitched to her chest. One day, she even cried to a Nazi officer: "dirty Kraut!" To which he replied: "I'm not a Kraut, I'm a man." Then again, the twins shared a language understood only by each other, a kind of personal dialect. The two H's didn't need to talk to one another to understand each other. The signals made by the one's body were immediately understood by that of the other, with neither brother nor sister needing to speak a word, or even to see one another. The fact of this singular language was overlooked in the case against the eldest. To my thinking, however, this language, which was precisely not their "mother tongue," is key. It could even be that the inability to speak a language belonging to a brother and sister born to her own mother had sharpened the eldest's desire to kill or cause the murder of her siblings. There was something else, too. The mother often repeated that her family was like the fingers of a hand. The expression made sense in this particular circumstance: three children, mother and father, which makes five. One couldn't separate the members of the family without dying. Implicitly, this dismemberment of the family unit was compared to a potentially fatal amputation: as if the severed finger—the separated and thus liberated child—could have caused a wound, a hemorrhage so severe that the remaining fingers would shrivel up, emptied of their blood, and would finally shatter like the dead branches of a sick tree struck by lightning. The meaning behind the adage repeated by this one-hundred-year-old woman was that no one could leave without killing the rest of the family, and in particular the mother, whose hands were after all quite beautiful, veined, and long-fingered. Or, equally worrying: one couldn't leave the others without dying. In fact, Henri né Bloch, however rebellious and sensitive, a man who, according to his twin sister, was the most artistic of the family and who cast an entirely singular eye over everything—who was, at least spiritually, the one who had always resisted—kept living close to his mother and was still staying with her while I was temporarily living with his sister. The father had never returned from the camps. For all that, in the family's mind, he wasn't dead. They had never mourned. Death held the living between its fingers. The dead finger kept the others prisoner. In other words, there was already a death in this mother's hand, but no one could see it. Not a single member of the family could recognize it. The deceased, it should be said in passing, was a remarkable man; but, unlike most of the remarkable dead, *he* had been remarkable while still alive. There exists written proof. And while he couldn't reasonably be held responsible for the fact, he was, by all appearances, kept at a respectful distance by the living members of the family. In reality, though, the survivors who, in their own refusal to grant the disappeared man his status as "deceased," found themselves contaminated by him. The dead man prevented the living from living; death robbed them of a full, open, and happy life. What remains of those who've gone before us is neither what they've said, nor what they've done, but rather everything that life sought to say and do through them, and that wasn't said and wasn't done by our ancestors.

Swim cap, bathing suit, and blue goggles all slipped down to the bottom of the plastic bag I had borrowed from my landlady. It was time to go downstairs and swim in the municipal pool located at the bottom of the housing project. I swam for half an hour, at least half of which I spent underwater, partly to work on my breathing, with the end goal of God only knows what test of endurance, and partly to observe, through my airtight goggles, the immature breasts (concealed by delicate pink nylon) of the numerous Chinese girls who came to the pool at this time of day. Then I got out. Silence reigned anew in the apartment. Hair still wet, I managed to slip a box filled with crumbs into the garbage chute while she had her back turned. Hannah née Bloch turned on the radio in the kitchen. The first time I had heard the presenter speaking, I had been surprised to hear a language that was Greek to me, but which, after a couple of minutes, I recognized as Hebrew. She listened to a daily news show broadcast from abroad over long-wave radio in the original language at the same time every day. This particular morning, the news program was following a debate on anti-Semitism in schools, on school walls, and in the minds of schoolchildren. During the time I'm speaking about—the period of my stay in her house—a series of reports was publicized about hostile acts perpetrated against the Jewish community. Updated daily with new samples, the list was read on air in its entirety. An anonymous letter was received at the synagogue in Varenne containing the quote: "the new market in Varenne will resemble Auschwitz with its watchtower." A red Star of David was discovered painted on the display window of a Descamps store in Mandelieu-la-Napoule. At 1:15 pm, April 11th, an anonymous call was made to a toll-free number: "You are a cursed race, you killed Christ, everything that's happening is your fault." A little girl was attacked in the metro; her attacker fled to Robespierre station, yelling "Supermohammed!" In Stains, during the Saturday service, individuals spread out around a Jewish place of worship bearing a large white flag featuring a closed fist and a gun, with the inscription "War/Darkness." The most common of these hostile acts was the appearance of that old Hindu symbol, the famous cross which has become known as the swastika, spray-painted, at night, on tombs, in elevator shafts, or on letter boxes in the project buildings. Buildings similar to the one I lived in at the time, and swastikas like the ones I could see in the metal cage of the elevator every day. These actions incited a permanent fear in Hannah, and inevitably took her back to the forties: that moment in her life when she had been just a kid, and the typical age to which (it is said) men and women regress, like the closing of a loop. So much so that during those conversations around the sewing machine, near the clay vase filled with homemade vinegar, those childhood years were eternally recurring. This woman always had her childhood (and thus, her mother) on her mind. They were all mixed up in memories of the war. Hannah née Bloch's thoughts carried the imprint of an historical period, while her skin's memory was occupied with the particular destiny of her parents. This internal, personal, singular scar determined her vision of life rather more than today's world did. It was equally true to say that she didn't invent the signs that made her believe that the somber period evoked by the list of events enumerated by the radio presenter was in fact yet to come.

When addressing an interlocutor one can always believe him or her to be rational, but one can never be entirely certain that this is the case. Hannah née Bloch's thoughts, her vision of the world, her Weltanschauung, were erroneous, partial, even absurd; but she was, all the same, entirely lucid. She approached the present candidly, entirely cogent, without the least trace of demagoguery. The overzealousness of her outlook and her pathological fear of imminent war manifested themselves less in her words than in the form that her words took. The way that fear would express itself through her in a sudden turn of the conversation was truly remarkable. What was striking wasn't so much her discourse, but the fact that in moments of terror (moments that became more and more frequent once I was able to notice them) her speech became marked with repetitions, choruses, refrains, which seemed to have nothing to do with the subject at hand but which, in these moments of fright, emerged, returned, were hammered out, and then ruminated upon in her mild voice, that of a mild, bewildered woman. Whenever a conversation brushed on an unrelated subject, Hannah née Bloch might suddenly insist that a homemaker's work must be recognized as a true profession; or that creating order in the home was a difficult, necessary task, which required real diligence. Or else she would again recall the love her immigrant parents had for the country from which they had emigrated. At the end of the day, it was possible that these remarks on work, family, and the homeland all came from that long-gone époque that her body kept bringing her back to, even though the ill wind of her refrain, however out of date it might be, contained at least some topical information, as she tried to convince me in front of the Singer table.

During these numerous and unexpected moments of worry, this woman's nursery rhymes were also occasionally about the earth's produce. Whenever she was throwing assorted leftovers into a certain jar, which had attracted my attention and which I would have emptied into the garbage were it not for its oversized dimensions, I would think of all these men and women who, amongst their memories of war, held onto those of hardship and rationing, of penury and famine. With the war over, they sometimes held onto all kinds of provisions, keeping them under the mattress—heels of bread, chocolate squares, chunks of apples—in order to exorcize hunger and, at the same time, to recall the hunger which had tormented them in days gone by. Those who had known hunger passed down the dread of hunger. It wasn't hunger that clutched Hannah née Bloch, though. As for me, I was well fed. I was thinking about a childhood without a father: time, memories that nothing could bring back, a crusty end of bread no bigger than a handful of rice.

It was now time for her to go to the market that would set up three times a week in the quartier where she lived, under a railway bridge. She would go beneath the tracks even more often than the retailers who set up their stalls daily, but not always under this bridge. It was a joy to her. Bundled up in an old Loden cloth acquired from a garage sale, and in winter with a de-feathered chapka on her head, her grocery bag made from tough material with a tartan print and mounted on wheels (a bag which would take the *bâtard* bread she snatched up with one hand further on its journey), Hannah moved down the length of the sidewalk with her incomparable stride: somewhere between *flânerie*, stationary stroll, and directionless march, however magnetized she was by a place and a destination. Her pace was a little slowed down by bad circulation in her arteries. She thought with her feet. Perpetually occupied with her daydreams, I mean that, instead of rubbing her soles against the ground, she floated. She had known many of these retailers for almost thirty years. I forget the last name of the fishmonger; his first name was Jean-Jacques, like the philosopher. The printed paper with which the cheese-monger wrapped up Roquefort, Tome, Laguiole, or chèvre ⸍

bore black letters on a blue background: Sobsczinsky and Sons. The year-round vendor was called Noah. From his stall, she would return with all sorts of vegetables wrapped up in large sheaves of brown paper. A word on Noah: she had told me once how this man, the erstwhile owner of an ass, had once made his animal climb to the second floor of his house, located in the prairie of Gresivaudan. Like a treed cat, the ass couldn't get back down from the second story: the strong men of the village had to rally together in order to bring the animal back down to its master's vegetable garden. The donkey episode really has no importance at all; I mention it simply because, during my short stay, it was told to me at least twenty times by either Hannah née Bloch or her husband. For me, the incongruous presence of Noah's ass upstairs is the incarnation of how our memory spurs us to ecstasy, steers us in two directions at once, and makes us balk. What's really difficult, even for strong men, is to hold onto the reins of memory. This episode recalls that other Noah, he of the mythical ark, naturally connoted by the presence of an ass in a room. In the past, Noah didn't stay behind the counter of his stall: he would place a small cup in between the carrots and the turnips and he would head to the café to drink a macchiato. The customers served themselves and put their coins in the cup like churchgoers of old, or like the people of today, putting coins into the tin cans in front of the hundreds of thousands of homeless, or even origin-less, people, now rooted close to McDonald's outlets, in alleys, and under bridges. However, Noah must have at least occasionally served his clients, since Hannah née Bloch got to know him. With two fingers, I pinch the tit then nibble the swollen nipple caught between my lips: handed over by Noah's generous hands and passed through the equally generous hands of his customer, a carton has moored itself in mine. Raspberries.

In her way devout, and beautifully and harmoniously shaped by biblical texts though she was, I'm not sure this religious woman realized that the name of her market gardener recalled the most beautiful stories of the Torah, which she reread each Friday. I don't think she did. As far as that goes, it doesn't really matter. The world of signs that she inhabited was coherent. She had no need to decipher this universe, as I was striving to, in order to pass the time, without ever really understanding why I did it. She had absolutely no need to interpret it. Like everyone, she lived in a singular space, full of signs and symbols, which were blindingly obvious to whoever came along, and which she, however, had no need to know how to read. The day of the flood, at the moment of the coming massacre, she would be saved by her friend Noah, transported on a ship full of her market gardener's beautiful foods, the vegetables like aquatic plants: fruits of dazzling colors, magnificent sizes, and incomparable scents. With these she would put together an altogether invigorating soup: victuals she admired while caressing Noah's apples, pears, or lettuces.

She draws up alongside the Garden of Eden. Sheltered from the violence of men, she goes to sleep under a walnut tree.

Except for going to market, she left neither her house nor her neighborhood. But, once a year, she would go to the anniversary ceremony of the camps. Having no taste at all for commemoration, she would do it to see old acquaintances again. That year, I accompanied her there. Like her, I found myself seated in the grass of a wasteland in the middle of a community of orphans. The official speeches took place outdoors without piquing her interest. Only a stele, half-buried in the green grass, along with the scattered debris of the bricks of the barracks where prisoners were once confined, reminded us that this field, where she now sat eating pistachios, had once sheltered a camp. According to the municipality's wishes, a parking lot had been built, eating into the former site of the barracks. They had managed to displace the site of the ceremony onto this wasteland but, according to what she told me, hadn't managed to put an end to the commemoration that was "harmful to the peaceful life of the city." I observed the old people surrounding me. I listened to their conversations. Hannah née Bloch had said very little to me about the child-in-hiding that she had been. Now, looking at these men and women around her, I suddenly realized that this gathering of humanity marked by time, experience, and age, was, in truth, a group of kids. This woman hadn't come to commemorate the disappearance of her father, but rather to laugh with this gang of feeble, once-abandoned children to which she belonged. This invisible community, though they were gathered in front of me in this meadow, only existed in the minds of these definitively solitary beings. Hannah came there in order to live out the experience of the child in hiding that she still remained. To find again the colony of wailing children within the bodies of the elderly people they had become. I realized then that I would never know the least thing about her childhood. She would never speak about this hidden place and time that were present and yet had totally disappeared. She had sometimes evoked life on the farm in my presence, the cows that had to be milked, the weight of the cans of milk that she had to pick up; once, she had spoken the name of the farmer who had protected her on a farm in Vosges. She had gone to see him again fifty years later and he had welcomed her warmly without recognizing her or putting a name to her face. Regarding this period of time, she confirmed only this: the children in hiding never spoke to each other. They spoke about neither where they had come from, nor why they were there, nor anything that could sketch out a family, brothers and sisters, nothing more specific than mentions of a life, a house or a father. Never. Most likely, these kids exchanged no more than the nearby animals did: calf, cow, pig. Thus, I had to recognize that this childhood in hiding would remain silent. The spell had eclipsed the reality of this time and place. As if her childhood had run to hide itself behind her signature expression: concealed behind her fingers, staying invisible to her own eyes and those of the world. I closed my eyes. I experienced for myself the child in the old man and the old man in the child, each blending into the other. Perched on my shoulders, I felt many men—more than a father—an entire generation, the same way that the former child in front of me felt the weight of millions of vanished people. Men made from the crumbs of men.

On the bus that was taking us back the city, Hannah née Bloch told me that only once in her life had she taken an airplane, and that had been to travel all the way to Israel. She had distant cousins there, and a birth had provided the pretext for this exceptional visit. Her mother, however, had made the trip many times over, in spite of her age. Once, in the heat of a terrible summer, forgotten on a suffocating terrace without fresh air, she had had a fainting fit; she had to be to be transported in an ambulance to the nearest hospital. In spite of everything that year, she didn't die in that faraway land; she didn't want to. Blind, half-deaf, she came back spellbound, overcome by the country's light and clamor. Unlike her mother, Hannah née Bloch, before the day of their flight, had never set foot on an airplane; it was something which filled her with terrible fear. So, she had never seen the sky or the earth from on high, except on television. She contemplated them from her window. Cosmos. White clouds. Mountains of snow suspended above the ocean, a sight that inspired a desire to be able to stretch out into eternity. For a week, she walked in the towns and villages. She recognized nothing. In the Holy City, in front of the Wall, she was amazed at its smallness, and saw in this stone construction only the shoring of the Dome of the Rock's promenade. She nevertheless slipped a little folded piece of paper into a crevice. Stones under water. Perhaps she made this gesture out of tradition, or perhaps in the way that she played the lottery every Wednesday rather than Saturday. She would hand her voucher to the newsagent who would slide it into a crack before giving her the electronic version of the little paper, which was then stuffed into the pocket of her wool jacket. Since the idea came to her at a moment when she deemed herself to have been fleeced by her mother—"not materially, but, above all," she insisted, "spiritually"—her playing this game testified to her wish that money would fall from the sky into her pocket, like a payment of damages. Or, more correctly, she made this gesture while dreaming that peace would come to her heart. A belief that she still hadn't given up on. The place where she felt entirely at home, at least seemingly, briefly (because she never set foot there again), was the bazaar. Without turning back, she sank into the shadows of the alleys. Without the cumbersome accessory of her caddy and the *bâtard* that could serve as a cane in a pinch, she started off without concern into the labyrinth, the lukewarm air lashing gently against her full face. She took joy in meandering between sacks filled with semolina, pyramids of oranges and bouquets of mint. In front of a mountain of spices, she stopped just to inhale the odor of the street, and beyond, of the region: she breathed in with all her being the sweet perfume of garlic and exile which permeated the air surrounding the carts of the year-round market. Further on, she argued in a language known only by merchants, and which she practiced daily underneath the railway bridge: the price of tomatoes, of oranges, and even of the mutton which she had seen behind the stall of the butcher with an altogether sinister-looking face. On a porch, standing in an alley, she was amazed to find herself face to face with a jar just like the one enthroned in her kitchen and which a seven-year-old child could easily slip into; in brackish water, swimming at the surface of the liquid, she discovered herring with pink, firm flesh, which immediately reminded her of Poland, where she had never lived. Amidst the motley crowd of this Middle Eastern area—in the flood of passersby wrapped up in their errands, everyone on the lookout for a colander, a toothbrush, or a pocket knife, she could, all the same, distinguish the old ladies who probably arrived from Central Europe after the war, who were above all recognizable by their way of pronouncing the Semitic language with Latin accents, but also by their faded European clothes, and by the little veins on the skin of their hands which didn't come from the sun of this region but, being grayer, seemed to be the stigmata of their western history—she found herself in familiar territory and at the same time on the margins. One moment, she felt deliciously at ease amidst the retailers whose first names, she believed, could be Noah. Cradled by a language with maternal accents, she all the same felt herself to be detached, apart from the rustlings of foreign intonations. Almost uncomfortable. It had already been some time since she had descended further into the labyrinth of alleys and shops. Was it in the corner of a shack lit up by a yellow lamp, the ground suddenly shining beneath her footsteps? The dizziness caused by the scent, in this nauseating place, from the stall that sold pastries flavored with rose, pistachio, and orange flower? Or was it the fact of knowing that in this spot, on this ground, with its mix of nervous matter, fish tails, overripe oranges, egg whites, men in black had not long ago picked up parts of a non-Jewish person's body with their white-gloved hands, identified twenty-four hours later by a propaganda tape as belonging to a seventeen-year-old Arab student in her third year of studying philosophy at the university? At this moment, baffled by the power of this nomadic exile that was born at the moment of her own birth, she felt her entire being capsizing. She was alone. Like her mother, Hannah née Bloch fainted. In spite of this dizziness, she reassured me on the bus, she had at no point been afraid there. In the bazaar, she hadn't thought of this violence, even though near the railway bridge, on the interlaced diagonal girders that the rail car rushed across at this moment, she made a daily trek in fear. She feared the freight train, which went by with a deafening noise above her, might explode, and she was also afraid of the violence between communities. Beyond that, at her core, she was gripped by fear of the war, which had already taken place and wouldn't start up again, but which laid siege to her memory. During that stay she was not yet suffering from the bad circulation in her left leg that would eventually prevent her from moving around freely. After her return, she never again spoke of emigrating nor of returning to that marginal part of the wide world. No. She remembered a bizarre country, where nothing conformed to how she had believed it to be. She had thought of it as a native land, without knowing exactly what that expression meant. Maybe she was thinking of the one from her childhood? Absurd. The Mediterranean countryside didn't at all resemble Vosges, where she had grown up under a name different to the one bestowed on her by her parents. Or perhaps she was imagining her father's portrait? We had arrived at the metal-and-glass door with its electronic keypad at the bottom of her twenty-one-story apartment building. She entered the code thinking of the name, Bloch. Impossible. A face seen for the last time at the age of seven could have nothing more to say to her now. With or without fear, the bazaar was the last territory on which she had strolled about with freedom and a brief but unadulterated joy, that of walking and of living.

When France took its lunch hour, I would withdraw into my room. The simple bed, a tray set up on two boards, an orange stool. Since dawn, I had considered what to do with this woman. For the nearly nine months since my arrival at her house, I kept track of what she did with her time, while doing nothing with mine. I spent a lot of time in the room in front of the double-glazed window. This time in particular, I watched carpenters at work on a neighboring roof. The Alpine countryside beyond. Then I sat down at the table. I had received an e-mail with a photo of a grandiose mountain range: an old friend had invited me to spend a few days in her chalet, located just over the border. When I came back to the living room, it was naptime. Hannah née Bloch slept peacefully in her rocking chair, an open book lying on top of her thighs: *Hostage in Jolo, Who killed Daniel Pearl?* or *A Complete Description of an Orphan's Life*. I am no longer sure which. I chose this moment to take my daily walk.

Leaving the building, walking along the street beside the metal gates of the municipal square, I bump into Henri né Bloch, my host's twin brother. He recognizes me and straightaway waves to me from the sidewalk on the other side of the street. I cross. He comes to meet me. Hunching for effect, he sits down on a bench. He says nothing. He is wearing a shapeless raincoat. Orange-framed glasses look me in the eyes. There we both are, sitting on the bench. Nothing else to do. I can hear his breathing."Track. Lottery. Bathrobe?" He offers a couple of words, reclining on the bench. Then, without any explanation, he takes a wad of photos from his gray overcoat. Extracts from his inner pocket numerous snapshots of a bygone world. These could be captioned: The Child in the Barn. A kid can be seen playing with wood in an obscure nook of the countryside. Winter is harsh. The boy passes his days by playing with cows, the fir trees, even the snowflakes that fall in front of the window of the attic, where he has chosen to make a home. In the distance, through the fog, one can see the harshness of the immaculate expanses, an icy wind breathes under a white light. The sun is masked by a thick stratum of clouds; it is a luminous halo. On the magnificent frame of the barn roof, seated with his back against a beam which smells pleasantly of wood, straw, and fire, the child uses a little knife to carve notches, make holes, bite into and, finally, pointlessly torture the hundred-year-old beam stuck in his eye. Like a three-card dealer, using the bench as though it were the flat side of a cardboard box, Henri né Bloch shuffles his snapshots. Then, like a gambler who is about to be conned but nevertheless goes all in, he seizes on one and flips it over. A kick sends the crate flying, and the world disappears.

Faced with these images of the brother, it appeared to me that whatever best captures moments of a man's life—childhood, when one learns; adolescence, when one studies; adulthood, when one works—does nothing to shed light on its entirety. I know from his sister that, in the darkness of the bathroom in the building where he occupies the same floor as his mother, every night he looks at photographs of people, portraits of men, jumbled scenes of humanity. Some of these photographs were taken during his childhood after the war; others date from other times, after other, more recent wars. But his period of creation came to an end when he chose to bury his head in his mother's handbag. And so, by night he goes back to look at the living eyes that he had captured earlier with his dazzling Polaroids. In his bathroom, he looks at the eyes of the dead, surprised that he is still living in the outside world. When we met at this bench, it had already been ages since he could stand the hundred-year-old bathrobe that scraped on the other side of the room-divider. Finally, a few months earlier, he had even gone as far as taking this spongy second skin of his mother's to plunge it into an acid developing bath, and then hung his living mother's bathrobe up as a curtain. That morning, as his twin sister discovered when she hastily came over, having tried in vain to get her mother on the phone (she was fast asleep), the empty article of clothing hung in the bathroom like a bird hangs from a branch in the forest. Its outside was shredded, in tatters, full of holes.

The brother suddenly took two walnuts from the pocket of his overcoat. His large hands, their fingers gnarled but fragile—the sort of hand that a young man could use to ask for a young woman's in marriage—were immediately put to work. He put a brown shell, and then another, into the palm of his right hand, and closed it. With the left flattened heel-to-finger against the right, he squeezed, like a worker cracking his knuckles, or, perhaps, like a poacher, come at night to strangle a rooster. Crack-crackkk. Then he opened his hand, looked at his palm, and saw the spectacle of disaster—the walnut's debris. Then with his free hand, he patiently separated the fruit hidden in the heap of earth, lying in the chaos. Of what had originally resembled an eardrum, there now remained, not the pretty outline of a musical ear, but two shattered, defeated, unrecognizable lobes. A mess of hard shell and oily flesh, the color of soft leather, enveloped in a fine, mottled-brown skin, fragments of which he removed piece by piece in order to bring them up to his mouth, eyes closed. Each of these nuts figured a piece of the man in his mute shell. Human debris lay in the palm of his hand. At my side, down the green felt of a Loden jacket, which was curled up in a ball on the bench, as if down a mountain slope, rolled the debris of Hannah née Bloch's brother's shell. After saying goodbye, I left.

More than ever, I had the impression that this man was the talkative double of an autistic person, unless he was the autistic double of a talkative person. Facing the slope, looking towards the projects, I thought of him. Although he had accumulated boxes filled with the photos of living people, portraits rivaling costume jewelry in their simulacrum effect, he had become a sort of negative artist, deprived of a body of work by life. In fact, he did nothing but pass his own in waiting for death, convinced of its imminence. He would even spontaneously shout: "My meter is running out! My meter is running out." Convinced, maybe, that his death was as deaf as he was himself. Every day, he undertook bus journeys, within the city and its suburbs, journeys that took him all the way to the end of the line and then back. Humanity thus transported— transposed—which he captured with his pupils, this was in some way his work. I had been re-discovered in his eyes a little earlier on the bench. When night fell, he could be seen sitting in the back of the bus amidst lonely men and women, smiling.

Upon returning to the projects, I was surprised to run into Hannah née Bloch's daughter. After she left, her mother and I had a conversation over pistachios. We were alone in the apartment. Entire fistfuls of pistachios disappeared beneath our fingers. This afternoon, as ever, she was thinking of her penniless but button-filled childhood: her uncle's material factory, sheepskin jackets, quilts, lingerie. Glove factories. To her mind, it was an orphaned childhood. The endless waiting for this father who persistently remained vanished. No news, neither a grave nor mourning. I listened to her while chewing. A prayer wheel. She endlessly unfurled sentences, without ceasing her pistachio munching. Everything led her back to the childhood in hiding that had followed the disappearance of this man; everything led her back to her mother. I floated. The mother couldn't see her daughter. She didn't recognize her. Hannah née Bloch tried to express her subjective truth to her mother. A vision that could take on the shape of her life, loyal to the way that life had given shape to her, and to the way that she saw the world. She wanted to give a name to the way she perceived her mother, who wasn't the center of her universe, but was a point from which Hannah née Bloch could think about where she had come and just maybe could find her place. The fact that she ended up thinking her mother couldn't see her testified to the enormous suffering emitting from her head, like hair pushing out invisibly, silently, lightly. The hair on the cranium appeared without sound. One day it would simply be there; its bearer wearing a helmet of pain. Weightless, of an unbearable lightness. Everyone, man or woman, carried the roots of their illness on their head, like hair of a particular color, texture, and growth pattern. In the end, a stubborn pain covers the child's skull. Hannah's pain laid spread out for me to see. I would look at the crest of her gray hair while she put a dry-aged shoulder of mutton or a free-range chicken into the oven. The gas stove didn't work well: the roasting tray was held together by a few sheets of aluminum foil slid between the body of the stove and the blackened grill, and it fell as soon as she put the piece of pink flesh onto it. The platter fell into the metal with a disagreeable sizzle. She righted the meat as much as she could. With a kick, I could have sent her toppling head over heels into the flame. After all, she was the terrifying witch incarnate, the mother nourished on chimeras. She immediately started up the prayer wheel again. At the same time, she nibbled. She did this in order to keep her hands busy, whereas I ate to soothe my mind. Or she, to calm her mind, and me, to keep my hands busy. It was better for me to listen to her blowing off steam than to let her head catch fire.

"She's the one who filled my head with rubbish. Like millions of children, I was lied to about my father's life and death, about my father's character, and finally, about my father's identity. I heard her once: it may be rare that a dead person returns, but the chance is nevertheless given, at least to some people, that's what I thought at the time, but not anymore. Mother succeeded in making me believe this impossible possibility—Father's return—by telling me that he had left, had managed to escape; she said that he had picked up stones, made a hole, put some pine cones over it—in short, that he had set up a trap in the earth, like the cunning fox in the fable. That he had survived, for some time. Someone other than he was dead, or rather, the dead person was someone other than my father. What did I know about it? As the years went by, I no longer expected him at all. My mother definitely pronounced the word "deceased" once—a word which sticks in the mouth of the person who says it like a kernel you can't swallow. We could never mourn. Everyone in this family lived on the back of the disappeared man, on the ruins of his death and, finally, on the spot occupied by a living person we couldn't bury. Without a sepulcher, no one could ever go to put even the smallest pebble on his tomb. "A pebble," she said, pinching a pistachio between her fingers, "which was destined for the soul of the deceased. When the dead man comes back to visit the spot where his body is buried, he can tell by seeing the little stones that he is still present to those who placed them there. Indirectly, if I can say so," she proclaimed, while digging into two more pistachios, "these little stones make the problems of the people who put them there even more current, more prominent, more human. Pebble mark here. At a certain point, without being able to precisely locate the moment in time (perhaps what is called adulthood?), I stopped thinking about death, no longer expecting my father's return. Since then, I have secretly hoped that he won't haunt me anymore. Mother betrayed me not only by not bluntly telling me that my father had been killed, she betrayed me because my whole life has been tied to the memory of this dead man, and ultimately, to death itself, to the extent that life has become an interminable mourning. In my mother's heart, I occupied the place of interminable mourning. Instead of raising me, her daughter, to face up to death, to affirm life, my mother trained me to recoil in front of life and take refuge in death's bosom. I told her this, once. And on that day, a Thursday, she called me a piece of shit. My own mother."

The 33 RPM cassette tape with the red label: diatribe; the last tape! "It's her word. She only used it once in front of me. Then she accused me of having soiled the family, betrayed my own. It's my mother, though, who filled my head with rubbish, privileging one version to the detriment of the other. My mother had a vision of things that was so domineering it blotted out everyone alive. Ultimately, her version was that of a widow. That her version became closer to that of our elder sister, denying the one shared by me and my brother, didn't really matter, even if I found it unbearable. My mother's so-called "survival" version was for me rather the fatal version, destroying everything, without care. We tell stories to help us live. The storyteller is sometimes attempting to save her own life. Mother always told an exaggerated version in order to live better, and she always presented it as the truth. But, it was only one version amidst other possible ones, the widow's version. For that matter, she modified her tale gradually over the years, improved it in order to keep surviving. Because I had to keep hearing this mumbo-jumbo, I got entirely fed up. Inside-out for so long that nothing could truly put me right-side-out. Since then, my life has been an attempt to level myself. Until the day when my mother's words seem null and void to me. With what magic, what luck? For a brief, merciful period, I could choose to pick up my mother's words or to let them slip between my fingers," she said, dropping the pistachio peelings, which, until then had remained piled up in the palm of her left hand. "Belief is ruptured. Really, for years she's been the one who isn't affected by what she says anymore. She mechanically unwinds the tragic thread, without being the slightest bit sensitive to the tragedy of life. As a result of protecting herself with stories, she's entirely cut off from our story. The child that she was, that she pretends is living, has become a corpse in her depths. Her stories were always fables, her own fables, murderers. But I've never seen a mother so well protected by everyone. At all costs, society protects its mothers. Even at the cost of its daughters and sons—absurd! A mother who produces daughters who no longer have any reason to live, who lack life and are close to turning back towards death, such a mother isn't good for society. On the contrary! Absurd! Such a mother negates the very principle for which society protects mothers: the perpetuation of humanity. Society forgets the fact that it acts against its own interests by protecting mothers who produce daughters who can't live. For everyone, the widow is immediately a victim. Society protects the widow more than the orphan. The State pays my mother a pension for my father's death. Bribes from beyond the grave. Widow, victim, pensioner? Kamikaze mother!" she ventured, attacking the final bowl of pistachios in a determined fashion. "She still dreams of finding her husband like he was the first time they met, young, virginal, but now a hundred years old. In order to live, she has to protect the secret that keeps her daughters from living. My mother is a poison to herself, to her daughters, and to society. But she perseveres in her existence, and everyone encourages her to carry on like this. Kamikaze indeed! Secrets, the unspoken, approximations, lies, omissions, little verbal side-steps—why not one person rather than another? An explosive suicide belt fastened around her stomach. A time bomb. She's carried around this dynamite her entire life, sticks of dynamite that threaten to explode her own body, blow up right in her face, commit suicide for her. She lived through a nightmare too. Some time ago, Mother sent her children to fight a losing battle, by pushing them into life without telling them about her own life, which paths she had chosen, if it's even possible to name such paths. In protecting them from the truth, a mother sends her daughters or her sons to fight a losing battle. Absurd! That's what I understood some time ago. The version told by the people who gave us life—that of our parents—is always the version of the dead. Better yet: maternity is death."

After her monologue in front of the gas stove, Hannah and I felt the heat of the fire on our cheeks. She had been preparing the sacred evening meal since breakfast of the same day, her words only interrupted by the silence that accompanies the lighting of a candle, before washing her hands. In the midst of all the victuals, saucepans, and napkins, she held her arms upright and only her hands busied themselves with their work. Separating the words …I meant to say the crumbs. A lapse of attention. After all, why not show myself the way I am now in the kitchen? Barefoot, fingers full of butter, my mouth full of crumbs. I relished it like a child in diapers licking the spoons abandoned by his grandmother. Precocious, that's what we were. In a time and place more than fifty years away, I had been the least loquacious in my class, she the most talkative. Or the other way around. As children, we were violently committed to games and laughter. In a fury, our bodies overactive, we stomped across our parents' living room, carpet, and bed. When we were done, we danced on our mother and father's bodies. The walls of their library hadn't yet tumbled down around us. We hadn't yet been stunned by the story that would later fall on us like a dictionary onto a skull. Toying with our parents' passions seemed without consequence, we were given the grace to disguise ourselves in their rags and laugh happily in the midst of their disaster. Time passed, we found ourselves defeated, amputated, bruised. We had to reconstruct, repair ourselves. Today, the mothers are imprisoned in their madness, the fathers impotent or vanished. The mothers always end up restless and mute, in wheelchairs at the ends of hallways in little

houses. We laughed. Childhood is an old master. A
sheet of sunlight fell on the kitchen tiles. I played for
a second with the last rays of sunlight. Trying to trap
the gilded dust-bunnies on the floor. But thinking
one can trap the sun is a child's game. Sun on the
ground is sun I can touch. It's alive.

The mystery of the jar now calls for an explanation. Hannah née Bloch poured wine, apple peels,
stumps of sugar cubes, and any leftovers into it. Numerous fruit flies flew around the vase in the morning.
At night, they were even more numerous, having been
born throughout the day. This vinegar was a perpetual
work in progress. Vinegar costs nothing—why make it
yourself? Everything ended up going into the mouth
of this jar, which never overflowed, even though she
would daily fill it right up to the top with liquid food.
Dregs that expanded marvelously as a result of chem-
istry, constant fermentation, and the uninterrupted
work of putrefaction. A vase as dangerous as a bomb
in her kitchen. This endless and bottomless mortifica-
tion could only have been conjured up by her memories, her childhood, and her mourning. Snippets of her
childhood that fermented deep inside her, and which
she hoped would eventually become recognizable to
her, rather than remaining alien to her memory. This
November evening, while she prepared the candles in
the living room, I decided to open the clay lid. In the

jar was a mother. A gelatinous membrane formed by fermentation on the surface of the liquid, it evoked the plasma in which a fetus is bathed. A viscous, slimy figure. A poison. In this way Hannah's concoction resulted in this edible, repugnant substance: a mother imprisoned in a jar. A putrefaction, that's what I had before my eyes, after she had spent months and years filling this receptacle with all sorts of scraps. The jar had given birth to a monster. At each meal, Hannah now used this potion to season Noah's aquatic marvels. She poured it into soup. She would finish it. However, she had another, more precise use for the mother. I discovered it two days before my departure. Before going to bed, she would extract a runny slice from the plasma with the help of a slender, sharpened knife, while her husband was swallowing his hawthorn-based concoction. Then, in front of her bathroom mirror, she would cover her face with it. That penultimate night, I saw her do it, through a hole in the bathroom wall that I had come across while bathing on that November morning. She remained unmoving for quite some time, with the translucent shape of the mother molding its features to hers. Dark, owl-like rings around her eyes, squashed nose, round brow. Her face disappeared momentarily underneath the gelatinous, living, organic layer. The metamorphosis she was hoping for—oblivion?—relied on this magical principle: a scrap or a spurt of eternity, in which her hands night after night collected the putrid, decomposed residue of this fantastical material. My eyes were riveted onto the miraculous jar. I had before me a depiction of limbo—the paradise of the mad—where the unbaptized, dead children and all monstrous beings resided. Contained within this vase, soaking the face of this holy woman every night, lived all the giants born as a result of a mismatch between the sons of the heavens and the daughters of men, embryos, the weak-minded, the prideful pushed to excess and suicide, imperfect works of nature, miscarriages, bizarrely mixed beings. It would take too much time to list all the others: idiots, bastards, twins, orphans, hermits; white, black, and gray monks, with all their frauds.

It's nighttime now. The first stars are appearing in the sky. I watch her praying. The gesture that she makes in prayer with both hands over her eyes recalls the one she makes to transfer the mother onto her face. Concentric and egocentric, formidable rotunda, throughout the day she never stopped beating the butter, sorting the crumbs, pouring wine, hardly moving from her spot in the center of her kitchen. In this space measuring less than nine square meters, and over a length of time spanning a full day, she runs an astonishing private marathon. It's only in this last little while of my stay in her house that her leg has stiffened entirely; a thrown blood clot. Bad circulation. Difficulty breathing. At night, her fingers become numb. Later (but I left before this) she could no longer move her feet or her hands. She carried on, though. Until her last breath, a head, this woman's head, never stopped stirring up her past life. Tirelessly, she kept on making vinegar out of her mother's back, she kept on eating away at the crumbs of her father, and she kept on beating the butter of her childhood. Autonomous, pendular, plant-based activity. Until the last day, the spirit of this admirable woman never abandoned her ethical, culinary work. Under her shawl, face tilted, she has her eyes closed. Her hands trace curls around the candles, carry the light of the flame towards her lips. She murmurs silently; an infinite grievance between her teeth. I have to face this truth square-on, I have life before me. That night, I experienced the never-ending sensations which once moved us, and which will continue to move us until our death. For a moment I felt the disturbance, and the continuation of our most fundamental thoughts, thoughts that turn us into children and that, up until our last moment, keep shattering us. In front of the picture of the red-crested rooster, Hannah née Bloch prayed to her god, the Rock. Swaying. Finally, I turned away. It wasn't about to end.

HELIANTHE NEE BOUTTETRUIE

HELIANTHE née Bouttetruie, now Wertheimer, was waiting for me at the station. Coal-black eyes, Florentine hair, pleasantly plump; she wasn't yet thirty years old. Her husband was there too. The couple had offered to have me stay for a few days in their mountain chalet, which they had acquired a year earlier. It sat in the heights of the mountain, above the lake, facing the slope. I had accepted their offer. Radical changes of scene, I mused, had long been my custom. I should mention that this particular time my friend welcomed me almost unwillingly. Not that she was ever less than generous, or that she ignored the laws of hospitality, on the contrary. Nor that she wasn't fond of seeing me. Quite simply, she was in the throes of a serious crisis. "Honestly," she had warned me, "I don't know if I can welcome you properly. The floorboards aren't finished," she clarified. The crisis she was caught up in was sufficiently worrying that in the last sentence of the e-mail I got two nights before taking the train, she had told me more or less this: "I am a sad soul who wanders in the ruins." As for me, I had hesitated to come, not wanting to be a spectator of a shipwreck, or for that matter, to witness any kind of storm whatsoever.

A crackling voice over the loudspeakers. Signposts. Connection. Direction. Exit. A small boutique with a lit-up display window containing a collection of multi-blade knives. An underground passage leading to the departure hall. Departure. A traveler's joy upon arriving on foreign soil.

Jammed into the back of a vehicle snaking along the bends, I looked through the sunroof as countless fir trees flew past, fixing my gaze beyond them upon the mountain peaks. I held out my arm, like a father leading the bride down the aisle at her wedding ceremony, to accommodate the Loden coat that was draped over it. I was thinking of an unfortunate episode from my friend's wedding. Hélianthe née Bouttetruie had been married to the young Hector Wertheimer for less than three years. In a small Protestant church in a mountain village, similar to the village we were traveling through now, the pastor, who was also the groom's father, had sounded out the groom's last name with the same pride and vigor with which little Ursli, of the Swiss fairytale, had rung his giant bell. He had droned on beneath the cold arches, his sing-song voice pronouncing each word as a separate unit. Having placed the ring on his son's finger, and barely completing the second part of the sanctified expression, "or for worse," he went off script: "Wretched. My son is a wretch. Wretched, good for nothing …" Cramped on the uncomfortable seat, I remembered Hector, squirming on the cushion of his prie-dieu, a few centimeters above the ground, suddenly shrunken, slumped, to the point of vanishing into the shadow of his father the pastor. The pastor was maybe not entirely wrong to rattle his son this way: the latter had gone onto disprove his father the pastor's ruling, when he, the unemployed wretch, found well-paid work just two years after his marriage, and he, the theretofore incompetent one, was soon able to invest in a mountain chalet. On this sacred occasion and blessed day, Hélianthe née Bouttetruie had burst out into raucous laughter: the pastor's tunic unexpectedly disturbed by his daughter-in-law's laughter, as though by wind on a suddenly stormy sea. "To leave behind anything other than deception and misery, one must be not a man, but a god, right?" I could make out the pink radiance of my friend's lips in the rearview mirror.

I disembarked, so to speak, onto a house in ruins. From the moment I came into the living room, with its menacing ceiling of metal beams in need of formwork, the place looked like a pigsty. My friend's house was certainly habitable. It didn't exactly resemble a roofless open-air pavilion, nor did it precisely look like a structure with holes for windows and plastic tarps for windowpanes, or like those houses we see in war-torn countries. It wasn't a house hailed upon by a rain of enemy fire, making its façade look like the face of a leper. The house wasn't situated in a warzone, in the theatre of operations, not at all. At the same time, it was clearly caught up in a war of sorts. At first glance, my friend's apparently well-organized and comfortable house could pass for a place of rest, even a refuge. On the other hand, it seemed like a construction site, a burrow, a rat hole even. A year earlier, on the telephone, she had enthusiastically told me about her chalet. "You'll see our farm. The walls are a meter thick; it's got at least twenty rooms." There were few windows and hallways. No garden. The village of G. where my friend now lived, seemed welcoming, but only when seen from the road in the background. In spite of its flaws, they could see either the mountain or the lake from the thin windows on the first floor of the chalet, according to which side of the building they found themselves on. A few months later, she had spoken to me of the same house with "disgust," her word, not mine. "I don't want this house at all, I never wanted to settle down in this region. I want to leave this country at all costs, to go live far away from this place, from these mountains and lakes." This is what she said several months after having bought a house needing to be entirely renovated, on which the couple had already blown hundreds of thousands of Swiss francs, equivalent to hundreds of thousands of euros. So much that they had been forced to take out a loan in order to make the monthly payment of another loan which had itself already sucked up both of their salaries. "I hate this house," my friend had declared immediately upon signing the necessary paperwork for the purchase of the chalet, where she now stood in front of me, in her half-demolished living room.

Hélianthe née Bouttetruie's father was responsible for the design of his daughter's chalet. Once a renowned architect, he had constructed buildings, hotels, and even churches throughout the region. He managed to be simultaneously active and moribund: a man who, on the one hand complained of pain and suffering and lived in his home as though it were a hospital; and on the other, was building things non-stop. Later on, he built only prisons and hospices. No doubt, his mental state wasn't without consequence for his activity. By destroying with one hand what the other hand built, he disrupted his own work. The plans drawn up for his daughter's house were wrong, faulty, and even absurd for a space that was meant to be lived in. Thus, after having conformed to the father's design and having destroyed a large number of the structure's interior walls, it was now necessary to reconstruct these same walls, to put them back up, simply to make the house habitable again. The construction schedule was appalling. No one could see the end of it. The worst was the flooring, which had to be destroyed, then rebuilt, then finally destroyed again, because of a design that was badly understood, badly drawn, and deliberately vicious. Aberrant in every way conceivable.

The father's design was disastrous, for the house and for the couple living in it. It was a destructive construction plan, not only for the architecture of the house—an ancient, rustic building with its own logic, even charm—but also for its inhabitants, who, because of this wonky design, found themselves living in the midst of dust, pebbles, and yellow plastic bags filled with detritus. Her young husband had done a lot of work to transform this pestilential farm into an almost comfortable place. After a year, the house was nevertheless a disaster zone, the couple was in ruin, and my friend, at the end of her strength and patience, her nerves frayed, was utterly exhausted by this life amidst the debris which had gone on too long.

Soon after my arrival, the couple really went out of their way to please me. Her husband went to chop wood. For the soup, his wife brought home all sorts of vegetables, bought from a gas station. The first night of my visit, she descended into the cellar and returned with a Serrano ham the size of a turkey, or even of a sheep, between her two hands. Strangely, she hung this piece of pork in the little hallway between my bedroom and the couple's. In the middle of the construction site, between them and me, was this acorn-fattened pig. It hung there in the hallway during the stay that, by discretion, I kept short. As I soon realized, it dispersed the sweet smell of smoked meat throughout the chalet. I felt immediately at ease. I cherished the mess straightaway, not at all bothered by the chaos, the debris, or the smell of meat. I've always felt well-placed in a room equipped with a bed, a table, and a stool, in someone else's home: every ill I would willingly wish upon myself can be found there. And if, by chance, I, Hadrien, were to have a family, I would ask for nothing more than to feel as at home in their house as I was in my own. Of course, I am no longer living in my own home in any permanent fashion. I was tired and I went upstairs, using the wooden step-ladder, to go to bed. That night, I slept like a baby, or a log. Thanks, no doubt, to the Alpine air.

"There exist countries that are sick; and there are thousands of reasons to leave whatever country one is, by chance, born to," the husband told me over break-fast, before mounting his international civil servant's moped. The region where I had landed seemed at first glance to be healthy, cheerful, and charming. In truth, it slowly worked on the bodies of its inhabitants, gently annihilating them, rendering them unrecognizable, and, finally, plunging them into despair. The couple had settled in this lost hole for reasons unknown to me when I first entered their home. From far away, this life had seemed enviable to me, like other people's lives sometimes, absurdly, seem better from afar. I admired their house in the country, the husband who would go have a drink with the local peasants, my friend who would travel every morning through fields and forests to the capital, where, as I had recently learned from the newspaper set down on the kitchen table, a distant member of my extended family lived and worked as a banker. He was pictured dressed as an Alpine hunter. Over slices of bread with cured ham soaked in a bowl of yellow *café au lait*, I learned the reason for their moving into this isolated house in a village perched above a lake. Hélianthe née Bouttetruie had moved to the mountains, she clarified, "to live close to her doctor." In reality, my friend hadn't chosen to live in this country, near her doctor, in order to be able to consult him whenever she pleased. It was rather the doctor who had his patient, in a manner of speaking, within easy reach, for her experiences. He wasn't in her service, as she pretended to think. She was a guinea pig among other guinea pigs for this incurable disease specialist, a Professor Baader. A piece of ham caught in her throat, she announced up front that she was suffering from a condition rare enough for it to qualify as a so-called "orphan" disease." One amongst a veritable nebula of mysterious pathologies," she said, making fun of herself and of her lot.

Aicardi syndrome, Von Hippel-Lindau disease, Angelman, Gilles and Tourette syndromes, Stone Man syndrome, Lowe syndrome, Marfan syndrome,

Retinoblastoma, neurofibromatosis, Ollier disease and Maffucci syndrome, brittle bone disease, progressive supra nuclear palsy, Addison's disease, Wilson's disease, leukodystrophy, melanocytic nevus, these varied pathologies have nothing in common except for their genetic origin. The symptoms are more or less of the same kind. In order, from least serious to most, the patient presents the following symptoms: firstly, fits of laughter, involuntary movements, grotesque facial expressions; then, the development of tumors, progressive general ossification, followed by the degeneration first of the cornea, then the retina, which reaches the brain stem and progressively affects balance, sight, mobility, swallowing, and finally speech. From childhood, the victim has extremely fragile bones. As a child, my friend found strength in the oblique and out-of-sync gaze she, perhaps unhealthily, turned on absolutely everything; as an adult, this same gaze made her experience an immense sense of fragility. Well-named, the orphan disease is lonely, without model or heritage. Arrived like the first person born on earth, without a known origin, like a traveler coming from a faraway country, without warning, from nowhere, errant, without roof or law, for all these reasons, the disease remains a puzzle for doctors. Of course, incurable disease specialists match up with orphan diseases. There is as much connection or relation between this type of researcher and this kind of disease as there is between an orphan and its parents, that is to say, none. The incurable disease specialist never manages to cure the orphan disease. Even more, only a post-mortem examination of the deceased's brain allows for a definitive diagnosis of the illness. One day, out of the blue, the orphan disease takes shelter under a man or woman's roof, and suddenly, his or her body harbors a new creature. Like a lone worm, the orphan weariness gnaws at the body of its host. Entertaining, how the orphan disease manages its situation, takes care of itself, if I can put it that way, by grafting itself onto the foreign body.

Obviously, the fact of its rarity had caused my friend's disease to be forgotten by all. As a child, Hélianthe née Bouttetruie had unwittingly housed this orphan. Then, since adolescence, since her first falls in the street, after stumbling while taking the escalator, had done so knowingly. Since then, the degeneration of bones that had progressively paralyzed her lower limbs made Hélianthe née Bouttetruie dizzy. It likewise sapped her spirit. Dizzy spells, falls, wobblings, she had had to endure them for years, and was subjected to them in waves, with higher frequency. All while nibbling on her piece of ham, she told me again that the orphan disease had "nibbled" on her leg. The left would from now on measure a good three and a half centimeters less than her right, giving her a limp, which she knew was permanent. Her mind fed on the illness, and vice versa. She was pathologically intelligent, capable of lightning-like clarity, but also bouts of lethargy, gaps, and disorientation. The orphan disease laid waste to her virtues: her vigor captured by a depth of absolute fatigue, her energy used up in vast misery, and sometimes in enormous disgust. In all, my friend displayed a warm, even friendly lucidity. She lived in this space where nothing ever got finished, finalized, or established. From there stemmed an unclouded mind, a will to destroy all beliefs. And humor, lots of it. She thought incessantly of work, an intense cellular activity, comparable to that of pregnancy, the embryo furiously developing in its mother's uterus; except that the machinations of my friend's brain were concerned with precisely that process, of (giving) life.

In truth, Hélianthe née Bouttetruie was destroyed. And I hadn't been slow to realize that the building was too. The owner's mood determined the verticality of the walls. Even meticulously cleaned, the main room could seem in disarray when my friend passed through it with her limp that was mental as well as physical. Conversely, if it was gloomy outside, and she was caught up in a busy moment of frenzied work, the light that emanated from her crazy enterprise brightened the day, sometimes even comically. At the times when she felt overburdened by the space, when she cursed the age, and hated her kin, her house, and even her own heart, she was wildly funny. Not long after her marriage, the fragility of her situation became legible in a look, a clenched fist, or the way a slightly tilting chair was propped up by a rug. She was now in an even graver state of destruction, ever since the doctor, that country doctor of incurable diseases, the specialist working on her case, the famous Professor Baader who lived a half-hour's walk from her house, had told her the night before my arrival that she couldn't have children. To be precise, he had issued the following warning: "Well, either you won't survive, but the child will live. Or else the child won't survive, but you will." To which he added, rather bluntly, "It is also possible that neither of you survive." The degeneration at work in my friend's body would, in the course of a pregnancy, be subject to aberrant genetic modifications that a doctor could in no way predict. During my stay, Hélianthe pondered the dilemma of Professor Baader's false alternative, which excluded another possibility that, strangely, they both rejected: that of life. As for many other sick people, rejects, philosophers, and monks, her pain and existence formed a couple that inhabited and doubled what my friend was producing with her body, her husband, or her house. This suffering was all at once an energetic salute, a wish and ultimately a will to live at once singular and endearing. Having stumbled into the rubble, her clothes covered in dust, her hair full of knots, she learned to accept it. She found strength in her unruly hair. I watched it wave out of the window of her car as we went down the road that led to the town.

I had met Hélianthe née Bouttetruie seven years before in a country inn. She was driving a red Mini Cooper then. She had become a close friend. At the time, I was renting a room in a furnished building, a sort of *auberge espagnole* in a country town in Italy. I shared this rooftop apartment with thirteen young women. A marvelous colony composed of a Finn, an Israeli, two Hungarians, an Italian, two Koreans, a Hindu, two Russians, a French girl from Beauceron, a Nomad, and my friend. During this stay, while I worked two dead-end jobs, whenever I had the opportunity, I gave free rein to one of my particular inclinations. Not obsessively, but with legitimate curiosity. What I mean is that whenever one of these young women left the house, I could go into her room, put my hand into a dresser, take papers out of a bag, run my palm over a silky dress, or the straps or cups of a bodice, even a finger or two over the part of an undergarment that was embroidered with Calais lace. If I found myself in an empty apartment, I immediately went after, in the following order: clothing, photos, papers. But the most coveted trophy was skin. Living apparitions of bent-over bodies, crouched while bathing, or looking at themselves. The bathroom was the appropriate place for this activity. I came upon all kinds of bodies in all kinds of places: my cousin's prepubescent body, seen shaking off in the pool; my grandmother's cadaverous body, seen shaking off in the hospital bathroom; the woman I had observed one morning washing her single breast, the other missing from her chest. This bruised apparition isn't the last one, even if it's undone. There were others. I have no name for whatever it is that moves me to do this. I, someone who was determined to never become a collector, have seen the most troubling, obscure, and subtle of collections. This ensemble of spied-upon women in the bathroom constitutes a vision of the living body from birth to death, from cradle to grave, depicted here by a bathtub. It's a fresco, a tableau vivant of the body's physique, where the epidermis of a mutilated woman is combined with that of a wounded, modern young woman: a tongue piercing, a diamond tacked into a belly-button, a ring looped on the lower labia visible from the waxed Mound of Venus. I've seen a blazing mother, an immobile, ecstatic old woman, and the cleft sex of a newborn child. I could have watched a naked prepubescent girl washing herself with a garden hose in the courtyard of her destroyed house in some war-torn country. I walked around my classmate Jean Glavieux's coffin three times: bulging eyeballs, pimply forehead, face swollen from the yellow drugs. I add to this my dead, and the deaths of those close to me who aren't born yet, visions of hell and mixed up limbs. They cling together like those I once saw in a mass grave. One Sunday I had crossed the border between Italy and the ex-Yugoslavia and found myself standing at the edge of a grave, half a cigarette in each of my nostrils to avoid the stench rising from the corpses: murdered men, buried, covered in mud and plastic shrouds, unwound and uncovered by gravediggers, in the opposite gesture to that of a florist wrapping a bouquet of roses in green tissue paper. After a little while, I tried to recover my poise. In this chalet, I hardly thought of these peeping activities and I respected the boundary between the couple's room and the one I was staying in without any difficulty. Boundary, rather than border, which for me was represented by the Serrano ham hanging in the hallway.

She had met her husband, who was foreign, in a country in which neither of them was born. Since her union with Wertheimer, Hélianthe née Bouttetruie never stayed still. They never stopped moving up hill and down vale. My friend's traveling schedule was impressive, travels motivated by an apparent disorder, and a schedule in fact controlled by her husband's transfers, assignments, and business trips. He was a specialist in bioethical issues: eugenics, discrimination based on the gene pool, the sale of gametes on the internet, embryonic cloning, surrogate mother services, organ trafficking, euthanasia clinics, medical experiments that contravene the dignity of human beings. A foundation sent him to various luxury hotels all around the globe in order to define universal precautions so as to prevent poverty from causing an unfortunate man or woman to sell a kidney, an eye, a child. At symposiums dedicated to these topics every year, he was tasked with formulating the legal regulations necessary to limit the practice of biological experiments, with an end goal of establishing a universal prohibition of human cloning. Hélianthe née Bouttetruie, now Wertheimer, put up with following her husband, joining him, and even welcoming him wherever he was transferred. So much so that if he was sent on assignment to Korea, she would sort everything out by taking a flight ahead of him, would spend a few days in Malaysia, and would pick him up from the airport in Bangkok for the weekend, then let him go off to a global summit on a neighboring island, finally meeting him the next week in a hotel which reminded her of good memories and where she would take it easy by herself. It wasn't unusual that they would find each other on the same day, at the same time, at the gates of the same airport. In the Arab Emirates, for example, heading to different destinations, they would wave to each other from either side of a soundproof window. Or, if they couldn't manage to find each other, lost as they were in the hallways or on single-direction moving walkways, they would try to talk on their cell phones. Many elements contributed to the frenzy of my friend's movements: she was afraid of being left alone, a fear now more acute than ever since she was living in an isolated house in an unfulfilling town; she knew the pleasure of moving across space, and therefore through time—distance, gaps, detachment. She had been living in exile for such a long time that she started to refer to herself and this exile as "we."

If it has to be explained, there is, according to me, yet another reason for her constant changes of address: an exceptional mastery of languages. Aside from her so-called maternal language, she spoke at least thirteen others. Furthermore, it's possible that her native tongue had been pushed aside by these thirteen others, that it had become a minority amidst all these other languages that she understood, that it had been shoved into its corner, one among many. She spoke and understood a number of these languages in rare dialects, like the patois of Munich, Friulian, or the

Savoyard jargon. Thus, arriving in a foreign country meant at once a new life and a new language. She experienced the joy of feeling foreign to herself, in the midst of her languages she was like a courtesan surrounded by her suitors. The surprise of hearing herself speak differently could make her believe for a second that she had chased her native, sick body from herself. In Italian, her clubfoot became charming. In German, her stiffness transformed into strength, or into farce. In Swiss-German, her handicap mutated into the ancestral defect of the village idiot: wild, raving mad, but also calm and maybe even happy, standing on soil surrounded by sheep. I've overheard her speaking with her husband, and the language changes several times in the course of a conversation. Are the names of languages the same in every language? Listening to their conversation making sudden leaps from one idiom to the next, I understood what it means to rise from or burst out of the bottomless hole over which all speech is forged. The fact is that, in narrowly escaping being lost in each instantaneous passage from one language to another—faster than a plane, a train, or a car—my friend experienced an aerial sensation, the feeling of floating on a flying carpet looking down over the wide world.

A new difficulty had appeared very recently. For several months now, almost every time he trod the ground of a foreign country, Hector twisted his ankle, pulled a muscle, or broke his leg. In the airports of Cairo, Ljubljana, or Reykjavik, where they still use portable walkways that pull up to airplanes while they're being refueled, he had several times fallen, toppled over, and found himself head-first on the ground. If Hélianthe accompanied her husband and was present for, but powerless to prevent, his fall, she would have to take him to the local hospital, where the doctors would give him a cast, splint, or bandage. If she wasn't there when he fell, but was rather in a neighboring town seven hundred or fifteen hundred kilometers away, as the crow flies, she would be obligated to take off and leave her hotel in order to rush to her hospitalized husband, who lay immobile and incapable of moving by himself. He was ultimately taken home in an airplane by his wife, to the house where I currently found myself. The art of jumping from the frying pan into the fire had thus attained its apogee, its apex, and its end. In a certain sense, her husband was truly an escape artist; my friend was the master of jumping into the fire.

These moves barely got in the way of my friend's work. Hélianthe née Bouttetruie worked without rest. She left the chalet in the morning, not returning until evening in a feverish state. She was hardly ever parted from her laptop. Living memories that she returned to on airplanes, on platforms in train stations, in bush taxis, as well as in rickshaws, palanquins, and gondolas. Her work, begun years ago at university, had seemed close to completion for years. She worked on memory. Not memory in general, but rather, the memory of war. She had absolutely no predilection for the theater of war, wasn't drawn to war-torn places at all. The classic family memorabilia, the stereotypical stories, full of cliché and somehow with the suffering endured by human beings pre-censored out: she had dismissed all of these from her field of research without qualms. She researched only those unavoidable stories that carried traces of the worry or perturbation that still troubled the writer's conscience. Working emotionlessly on this scorching, awful, despicable material, this is what she was committed to, this was where the true difficulty of her work lay. More difficult than researching, than collecting, or even reading this terrible material. The object of her work was time and the event. A present that obliged one to rethink the past. A scar: the mark of suffering, of pain, or illness which no longer exists, but whose trace remains visible. She worked on her subject like Moses. She in no way considered it charitable or moral work. She looked on with a coldness like that found in Ernst Jünger's *Journal of War and Occupation*, barring maybe the moment when he learns of his son's death. "Even then," Hector, who was reading the work of this dead, one-hundred-year-old German, said to me during my stay at his house. She showed the pain, both past and present, acknowledging to herself that she was filled with a sickness which she didn't show, or only did during those bouts when her body, attacked by this degeneration which caused one of her legs to shorten, would suddenly begin to tilt miserably, like a stool or a chair which has one leg shorter than the two or three others.

Not far from the chalet, three days after my arrival, an innkeeper found a bag at the edge of the lake. The bag contained a handful of fetuses, which were later identified as the only children born to a single mother living in "human misery," which is how the radio presenter precisely put it, in a drawling accent. I have no idea how my friend took this crime in her heart of hearts. Later that morning, she nevertheless started talking to me of children. She said: "Children die sometimes. Abortions, poor sick little things carried off by death, as if the death that came before their birth has robbed them of life. It's not their own death, not a dying born from living, a friend accompanying them through and carrying them away from life, but rather a death originating from older generations not giving their successors time to arm themselves. This death is a harpy; from a distance she harpoons the newborn, who in one blow is robbed of ever attaining adulthood, but also of fighting against its own death. Sometimes this bad death carries off adolescents, who hang themselves against their will. It's rare that any of them manage to live. If they reach the age of adulthood, they still never become adults. They are glittering corpses. Yes. Glittering corpses. I'm afraid of this death that captures innocent beings, grabbed by the hair without warning, born with an ancient death at their side, the deaths of all their ancestors who, since the nighttime of the world, haven't said what they couldn't speak."

That day, she stayed at home in the chalet with me to let the plumber in. Up until now, in order to bathe, we had had to heat cold water in a soup pot on the stove, or use the icy jet of cold water in the courtyard, if one could stomach the glacial cold. Two illegal workers showed up in front of the wooden double door. In an Italian accent, the first one, who seemed to be a Portuguese immigrant, later told me that he had been born in the Ukraine. The other, his helper, exhibited a hole in the middle of his forehead. Though shy, he had finally told my friend how he had been forced to leave his native country, Algeria, after being arrested at a roadblock and left for dead by a militiaman. This man had pistol-whipped him in the forehead. Blood had immediately started to flow like a fountain, flooding his face. Knocked unconscious and seeing stars, and then coming to, he saw a second militiaman through the blood that continued to flow from the hole in his skull. This second man was anxious to finish the job without using up too much ammunition. The mercenary fired into any moving bodies on the ground. Motionless, face protected by a puddle of mud, the man had been left for dead while still alive.

It took several people and two tries to lift up the equipment necessary to de-lime the boiler. In the course of putting the equipment together, the two men brought a plastic container the size of a jerry can into the chalet. It contained a combustible, a liquid detergent not to be left within reach of children (not a problem here) and a portable motor. This was used to activate a pump: round, metallic, dirty. The whole thing looked like a welding rig, or diving equipment. Instead of connecting the whole outfit to the body of the heater (something prevented by the lead pipes concealed at the back of the device, which had attached it to the wall for decades) they installed the circuit in the following fashion: from one side of the pump, they affixed two plastic pipes to two taps that had earlier been removed from the bathroom; from the other side, they joined the machine through the opening of the container filled with the liquid treatment. Then there was nothing left to do but turn on the motor and wait.

The liquid passed through the cold-water tap in the bathroom towards the circuits in the hot water heater, traced a path through each of the pipes in the device hanging from the wall and came back out through the hot-water tap in the bathroom, towards the machine. Its role? To digest and then redirect the liquid towards the ailing appliance. Imprisoned in the closed circuit for several hours, the liquid product efficiently did its job, taking off the layer of lime that had accumulated in the appliance. The plumbers spent the rest of the morning chatting. Beneath the living room's menacing ceiling, they savored a tin of flaked tuna in olive oil for a moment. During this time, in the bathroom, the hot-water heater cleaned itself all on its own. Invisibly, the corrosive liquid did its job, eating away at the lime scale. Eroding, carrying off clots, minimizing cysts. Unceremoniously destroying.

My friend daydreamed while watching the invisible circuit of the liquid treatment in the appliance, thinking of the machine of her own heart and body. Her gaze passed over the countryside through the chalet's windows. She saw the ghost of that Bin Laden man for a second, carrying a dialysis machine mounted on a donkey through the snow-covered mountains of Peshawar, the donkey devotedly led by his loyal doctor, Ayman al-Zawahiri. A true son of his family, his clan, his tribe, and his nation, chased from his nation and even deprived of his nationality. The emir and his loyal lieutenant progressed towards the mountain ridge of Tora Bora and the emir's donkey carried the blood-cleansing device on its poor back, the device necessary to his survival. And behold, Sancho Panza and Don Quixote leaving La Mancha, men indeed capable of transforming the twin towers into windmills of death. Now night falls, and in her reverie, my friend again makes out the Knight with the Sad Face at the back of his cave, the dialysis machine connected to a generator that his loyal doctor, pedaling in the twilight, feeds with the sweat of his hairless thighs. Hélianthe née Bouttetruie thinks about this miracle. Exchanging blood is the object of her prayers. Not just like in simple dialysis, though. Not even to cure her kidneys, or banish the orphan disease. Just to live better. To give life, stop limping. She too wants to create a lineage, to find her roots, establish filiation. Giving life is the chimera she chases after, as others chase after other chimeras. To each their hobby.

At teatime, we had a visit from Wertheimer's youngest brother, who lived close by. Bent over as though he was climbing the mountain with his flock, his hands on the collar of his green felt coat, he showed up at the chalet. Exhausted, bowed over, grumbling, he was still looking around for his animals. During his adolescence, after returning from a trip to Mexico, this belated and distant brother born to a different father was struck by melancholy. At the time, he proclaimed to anyone who would listen that his parents were his best friends. He had no others. He had been working for a while as a bagger in the big supermarket located in the valley's industrial zone. He filled the customer's bags up with the customer's things. He lived without a wife. Later on, he found a farm up on the mountain. He became a shepherd. Since then, he'd been barely making a living off the Alpine pastures, in a mountain hut perched higher up. He had bad character, was bad humored, and even foul-tempered. At his brother's wedding, seated at the table of honor with the parents, in-laws, and grandparents, he didn't unclench his jaw once during the entire meal. Want to know why? His hut was on a hill that was 1,730 meters tall on one side, and 2,063 meters on the other. A shepherd who doesn't have a good dog plays the dog himself. He played the dog. He was at the end of his rope and fit for the loony bin. To brighten his days he would stretch out on a rock in the meadow. He was soothed by valleys (his older brother was calmed by violins).His mountain hut was his refuge. The view of the fir trees did him good. He played with pebbles all day. "I don't think about anything, I don't feel anything," he would say. Then he would toss a stone. In the sheep pen, he would sometimes mutter: "My life is lousy." Other times, he would mumble, "Childhood is a stone deep within you. Go look for it." Then he would throw a pebble up the hill. "Death is my stone," he drooled, nose in his soup. And he would go back to watching stones hurtling down the meadow. He would ruminate in the heights, on the slope, for entire days. He spent years in the mountain pastures, cloistered in his hut, looking at the rope attached to a beam above him, always within easy reach. Exactly like here. A dog barking in the distance. A man's life. The shepherd of Cock's Hill. "All the sheep that go into the abyss," he would suddenly stutter, and then trail off. In the black night, the brother left the same way he had come, without saying a word, or nearly, but after having swallowed a good dozen slices of cured meat and emptying three very nice bottles of Fendant de Sion.

All the while telling me about her husband's unfortunate brother, Hélianthe née Bouttetruie led me by the arm towards the shed outside. She had stored her grandfather's paintings there. On the threshold, my friend had reproduced the adage that her grandfather had carved into the wood above the door of his studio: *"Cum hominis vocabulum audio, mox accurro."* Pinned up at the entrance of the shack, on the left, I could see a little black-and-white portrait of the painter: jolly face, pale complexion, a mysterious smile. Sprawled in a rocking chair, right in the middle of his studio, he, bizarrely enough, held a jar filled with bank notes from the Bank of France. In bills with large denominations. "A prize he received, belated recognition," clarified my friend. "He painted in secret from the age of fifteen. My grandfather grew up in a community of his parents' and grandparents' friends who found sustenance in books. Everyone lived right next to a huge library. The books may well have been read, but he was struck by the extent to which they had nothing to do with the lives of the people who had supposedly read them. Maybe the library was an alibi, my grandfather announced one day. Anyone who possesses a library is a book collector, not a reader. Anyone who spends all their time and their life in the service of art isn't an artist. He was repulsed by dilettantes of art. From an even younger age, he had rubbed shoulders with amateurs, pseudo-artists, people who collected mechanical music boxes, painted, wooden Russian dolls, pornographic photos. 'All those freeloaders!' he had pronounced. When you looked closer, the music box collector was crazy, but the worst one was the relative that his mother, my great-grandmother, had a crush on: he collected circumcision chairs. My grandfather once confided in me that in a way, this man's collection, his art, in a manner of speaking, was strongly anchored in his pathology, and thus was more closely related to the truth of those who use beauty to redeem their pathetic existence. Later, when I was little more than fifteen years old, my father, his son, who had inherited this collection, invited me into the smoking room one night to sit on one of these notorious circumcision chairs, the pig!"

I looked around the meticulously tidied studio. Canvases covered all the available wall space, and the remainder were stacked up against each other two or three deep on the ground. "My grandfather was a horse of a different stock," she continued. "He started from scratch. The only question he had for other artists and thinkers was about their material situation, the economic conditions of their production. He would point out that lots of talented artists and innovators are the children of bankers, and even when they aren't, they're fed, washed, and given a roof by their parents. If my grandfather met an artist or thinker, he wouldn't want to speak with them about their art or their philosophy. The only question he truly had for them: where does the money come from? 'I have solved this quandary,' he once declared. He believed that caring about life and asking questions about money were one and the same, as is revealed by the expression, 'means of living.' It seemed to him that a successful artist or thinker was one who had resolved this problem, who no longer had to ask the question. The successful artist earns a living and plays with truth, nothing more. That's what my ancestor confided to me one night while I was playing with pebbles on the floor of his studio." My friend wandered, limping slightly, between the few sculptures made by this man: tree leaves made from green felt, improbable contraptions, stumps of men, all of it without embellishment. "The old man had a singular, prodigious knowledge of painting," she continued. "He particularly appreciated unknown painters. A couple of times a week, he would go to visit some people who painted in their barred rooms in the asylum not far from his house. My grandfather knew the history of art, knew about the lives of the artists he respected, but he also knew about the most unique methods of creation: cave paintings, Arabic maqam, sand drawings, puppet theater ... He was equally conversant in the basic elements of painting: paste, subjectiles, strokes, pigment. Wiping away all the ridicule, the mockery, the insults the same way he wiped his paintbrushes every night after work, he painted without stopping. Yet, his confidence in the work that preoccupied him was equaled only by his anxiety about the piece that he was working on. Since the beginning, this feeling had never lifted. He only ever agreed to show a painting after great hesitation. The result: a true body of work, with styles, color experimentation, geometric sequences. He only left out self-portraits. Because of modesty, lack of confidence, inability? I don't know," my friend added with a pout. "As for me, I admired his work, but couldn't at all grasp such a powerful vision of the world. Later, I was able to discern the eras of his works, wherein everything made sense, not directly, or deceptively, but as the art of a powerful painter immersed in life: I found his life and the life of the era fused in his work. However, he was lacking something. My grandfather never took time off. Every night, he shut himself into his drawing room. He never again left the damp walls of his studio to go walking in the mountains, as he would sometimes like to do with me. He was doubtless holding onto the memory of cold stony ground trod at dawn, the morning air when day breaks over the gray-slate roofs, the walks with his sketch notebook, over the sloping meadows, the grassy green hills where he would watch the cows grazing, like Roger Bissière did in his time, when he had renounced painting before accomplishing, nearly blind, his most luminous work. My grandfather no longer perceived the border between creation and repetition. He couldn't distinguish the boundary between work and inactivity, nor could he see the chasm between shape and infinity. The more he worked, the less he knew the tranquility of the artist who declares: 'I'm at work when I'm doing nothing,' though he repeated it often, citing Fernand Léger. He no longer saw the difference between creation and extinction. He carried on endlessly. Right up to his end." Hélianthe née Bouttetruie was now rooted in front of a canvas depicting a rooster. "Who can say what a successful artist is? Would he be a successful man? My grandfather asked that not long before his demise. Then he died. Goodbye all! I could say that the old man had all the artistic qualities and all the human qualities that a man and an artist can possess. Honestly, I can't name anything he was lacking. Maybe nothing? Nothing but a little joy (in life). All the same. As an artist, he was an orphan of truth. He had art to heal himself of truth."

Leaving the hut, I glimpsed a little wooden shelter not far away on the hill. Below, in the sloped meadow, I had noticed a sort of groundskeeper's cabin, where the farm's erstwhile facilities could be found. I headed towards it. No doubt in order to experience the cold, the amazing voluptuousness in the asshole, the pleasure of feeling oneself over the pot, from which emanated the musty smells of an uncovered pit, the power of this mountainous, Hercynian terrain on top of which the country cabin rested. Almost equal to a bottle of Fendant de Sion. I went in. The smells of the countryside rose to my now-chapped lips. Squat toilets. Even more rudimentary: a rotten wooden floor, a hole drilled into the middle, scarcely anywhere to wedge your feet on the worm-eaten edges. I squatted. At eye level was another hole, an orifice in the wooden dividing wall that I hadn't seen when I first entered. This crack let you view the summits while you did your business. I saw pastures, hilly enclosures, flat, rough stones. Passes, crags, peaks. Chinese puppets against the gold-rimmed sky.

Late the next night, Hector had a moped accident. He collided with a fir tree on the road, a hundred meters from the chalet, a little beyond the museum of agricultural machinery. Incidentally, fatal accidents often take place one hundred meters from the victim's home. Their hearth in sight, the man or the woman gives into their accumulated weariness and half-shuts their eyes. The road is familiar, the driver is not paying much attention. At least, it seems right that the possibility of coming home again turns people into road hogs—they proceed recklessly rather than in a straight line, taking shortcuts, driving more dangerously. Despite the appalling cold, the alcohol Hector had ingested kept his body at a reasonable temperature. When emergency services (either Red Cross or Saint Bernard) got to him, he was abashed, but living and tolerably disfigured. The moped was destined for the scrap heap. During his brief stay in the canton's hospital, he was allowed to receive in his room in this order: the police, his boss, then his wife. The police told him that he was risking a sentence of three years in prison, without stay. His boss came to reassure him of his support, though he also mentioned the fact that the police had informed him of his colleague's worrying level of intoxication. His wife came to take him home. Hélianthe née Bouttetruie, now Wertheimer, had offered up all kinds of reasons to explain her husband's accident to me: fatigue, problems at work, and even alcoholism, explanations that weren't in the police report. I had in fact noticed that my friend's husband had put on a little extra weight in between our first meeting and this stay at the chalet. I had supposed that the dry white wine drunk every evening in the company of some of the villagers contributed to his well-padded, puffy appearance, as though he had put on a big, wool sweater knit by his grandmother underneath his white international civil servant's shirt. Several mornings, I had come across him in the kitchen, unshaven, disheveled stubble on the bottom of his face and neck. Head visibly swimming. After the accident, he stayed home. Hector said that he no longer knew where he was, that he hardly recognized his name, and couldn't figure out what he was doing there. He now spoke in an incomprehensible gibberish, a mixture of all the languages he had learned. He stayed in bed in his room all day. Hélianthe was worried about his condition, but said nothing more to me about it. Could she have? Hector called her name. She had to go upstairs. I soon found it necessary to leave my hosts. From afar, it simply seemed as though the couple had been buried.

The last day I saw Hélianthe née Bouttetruie, she was collapsed on the rubble in the living room, underneath the metallic girders that seemed suspended in the void above her. She was contemplating the designs her father had left, written out on scrolls in every direction. A clutter of lines, dashes, and abstruse terms. Plans that had revealed themselves to be disastrous for her house, her marriage, and for herself. She now ripped up these scrolls in front of me. Mechanically, her fingers tore up the big sheets of white paper into different-sized pieces, which she tossed onto the ground and brushed at them with her short leg, like a school child wipes away letters on a blackboard, or like someone walking in a graveyard, and, wanting to read the name of the deceased on a gravestone covered in snow, swipes a foot from left to right, in order to uncover the letters carved into the marble and now buried by winter. In front of a destroyed wall face, Hélianthe née Bouttetruie whispered that she could never give life. She was only good for "passing on death." Coming from her, this statement seemed doubtful.

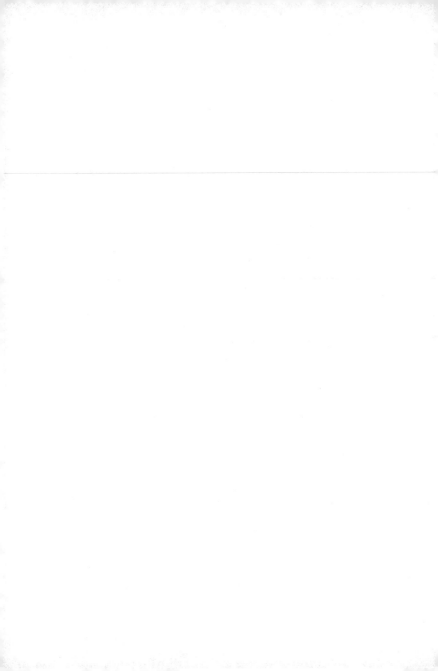

HENRY NE BERG

While I was walking on the path that overlooked the lake, as I did each night, taking the trail upstream from the chalet, I was thinking about the distant member of my family on whose name I had landed in the middle of the salmon-colored pages of the local paper, from which I had learned that he lived not far away. At the time, I had considered respecting this coincidence and going to visit my cousin out of courtesy, while also taking the opportunity to get away, getting physically further from my friend and mentally closer to this man. Killing two birds with one stone. Actually, I had once felt a distant friendship with this man; from afar, I had offered him my admiration and understanding. In the end, I had felt sympathy towards this character who, as far back as childhood, I remember as having never addressed a single word to me. No matter. I would doubtlessly have been a total stranger to him; he wouldn't have recognized his remote relative. To be totally honest, he wouldn't have been able to put a name to my face, and I wouldn't have been able to put a name to his. The poor man had long ago lost all use of language. So what good would it do? He was the only relative for whom I felt some respect. Not for any particular reason, but precisely because he had nothing in common with my parents. The last time I had seen him, he had been lying on the bed, back on the mattress, his legs propped up, and his feet resting against the wall, his head upside-down. That was years ago. Seeing him lying there on the bed like that, doing nothing, his feet propped up against the wooden partition, I couldn't imagine what he was thinking about. What was his teenage dream, what would his adult one be?

HENRY né Berg had decided to cut himself off from his parents while they were still living. He planned to dispossess them. To take off with the inheritance. Something I didn't know about then. Of course, from this moment on he gave off the impression of extreme confidence. An emotion he hadn't always felt. As a child, steeped in utter anxiety, he decided one day that this was after all good luck, more powerful than confidence and that he had avoided, as much as possible, sinking like a stone, losing control, even hanging himself. "Anxiety and confidence are two sides of the same dynamic that inexorably drags man to his death," he declared one day, addressing his bedroom ceiling. Was he, perhaps, carried away by an instinct stronger than death? Even from a very young age, Henry né Berg seemed confident in his intentions. Head upside-down, lying on the bed, he bided his time. His project occupied his mind. At the same time, he wasn't in any hurry to complete it. For years he had perfected a project that he felt no urgency to execute. For a long time, an aristocracy of will had made him think of the fulfillment of his will as a mere trifle. He attentively examined the acts and gestures of his predecessors. Detecting nothing new or vital, he wasn't in a hurry to do better. He wasn't at all inclined to sacrifice his project for its achievement. Process took precedence for him. He dreamed of the perfect gesture. All the same, he was disappointed by his own inaction, which reminded him of those years where, as a child, he had, like an autistic person, willingly stayed in his parents' basement.

Brown-haired, straight-nosed, with the refined face of a refined young man, I see him seated on the bed, feet against the wooden wall, smoking nonchalantly. Henry né Berg was a boy I spent time with while I passed the winter in his mother's chalet. His mother was neurasthenic and even genuinely sick. Regarding his father, my cousin often repeated: "My father had no sons. My father had no sons." A sort of orphan. He only went into his house by the service stairs. Dragged along by a female companion, he was reminded of the monumental steps of the main entrance of the mansion that his mother and father owned and lived in, like the steps of a palace where he would arrive as a foreigner. After a long trek, he rang the bell on the heavy door of his parents' house, as though he were entering a monster's den, at the edge of a thick forest, far from society, from all human life. Like little Hansel, misdirected into the forest by his own mother, who, from between the bars of his gingerbread prison, gives the witch a bone stripped of chicken flesh, rather than one of his own fingers, hoping to postpone being killed. Henry didn't need to hide behind a chicken bone. But the story I refer to has nothing to do with this children's tale.

In the attic, in his childhood bedroom, objects were arranged in apparent order: a pair of skis leaned against the attic wall, the pair of handcuffs hung up on one of the pipes of the cast-iron radiator, the pair of binoculars sat on the desk. Very early on, he would settle in to doodle at his table in front of the small, circular window. He sketched out the details of his plan. First, in trying to come to terms with the riddle of his childhood, then the riddle of his adolescence, and finally in reconstructing the riddle of his prison, he had contemplated his project from a young age. While he was copying down the dictation on the "question of God" read to him by his father, he filled up writing notebooks that his mother obliged him to fill up. These exercises were early drafts of his anti-parent project. Occasionally, he polished his shoes. The rest of the time, he stretched out on his bed, legs against the wall, and stayed there doing nothing, sometimes for an entire day. Head upside-down, he stewed. Eyes closed, he pondered. At the end of every week, his father would come to check the boiler's fuel level in the ex-stable, located in the back courtyard of his parents' mansion, the attic of which was inhabited by Henry né Berg. In this way, the father could get a precise idea of how much his son was costing him. No doubt this gesture led Henry né Berg to execute his plan. He must have been dreaming of it while his father chased him from the living room, imploring him not to walk on the Persian rug and to use the service entrance. Unless he came to his decision because of the crumbs that his mother (in collusion with the baker on a neighboring street) would bring home by the bagful, from which she would then extract a fistful that she would weigh herself before having the nanny mix the portion with tepid water, a soup that her son ate all alone at the head of a long table in the office.

I walked. Fifteen or so meters ahead of me, at the foot of a fir tree, was an animal lying on its side. A red, black, and hairy mass. From what I could distinguish of it, one eye was half-shut while the other was half alert. It hadn't moved since I had appeared on the path. From far away, the thing brought to mind Henry né Berg's father's dog: a creature connected in my mind to a felt pelisse, hunting coat, and mountain blanket. The Loden coat would lay over the old man's knees like a relic, at the edge of which lay his dog. Lit by the fireplace, man, animal, object, all three formed a single body, a seamless blend of wool, vegetable, and something barely human. Mechanically, the father, almost immobile, felt beneath his fingers the coarse and the soft, the dainty and the heavy, the silky and the rough, the wrinkled and the smooth, the felted and the granulated, the gentle and the prickly, the shiny and the rippled, the fleece and the down of the combed sheep's wool of his Loden. After the hunt, the banker would return, his coat stamped with an acrid, animal smell. He systematically scraped off the snow and mud stuck to his boots on the sharp, metal blade attached to the stone in front of the mansion's entrance. Preceded by his dogs, the arrival of the father, head covered in snow, dressed in his down coat, somber and twinkling, was a moment of terror for his son, caused more by the noise of the pack than by his so-called progenitor. Having climbed up to the animal, I tossed a slice of smoked meat that I had kept in my pocket towards his snout, where there gleamed a row of fangs covered in a coating of white saliva. He let me continue on my path.

Before becoming a man, Henry né Berg had wandered about aimlessly for some time. Since adolescence, however, he had chosen to work in his father's bank. He gained admittance to the bank that bore his father's name, armed with limitless confidence in his own lucky star. For years, he had been content to remain a simple accountant working for the Berg bank. If he had been liked, he would have inherited the family business. Would have been his father's successor. The father had, as they say, declared his son to be the heir-apparent. While taking no pleasure in the task, Henry né Berg's father would have helped his son climb the business ladder, leading him by the hand, in a manner of speaking, until he reached the pinnacle of the business. And then would have crowned him. Declared the heir by his living father, the son would have taken the crown from the hands of his father's ghost. With the father's ghost giving him the knout instead. When Peter the Great's son, Prince Alexis, received a knouting at his father's hands, it was the son's hands that trembled, not the father's. In any case, the fathers were once sons and the sons would be fathers. Even without sons. Following the schedule that he had imposed on himself, despite the trembling of his hands, Henry né Berg was not afraid. After years of silence, spent rummaging through his client's safety deposit boxes in the bank's cellar, he set about disinheriting his parents. Such an undertaking called for talent, competence, and obstinacy. The dispossession of his parents was neither a benign gesture, nor one without consequences. Such an act couldn't be done with impunity. He prepared the dispossession with a number of lawyers, notaries, and consultants. However, his intelligence was the main key to this scheme. He prepared for this act first of all with his mind. Henry wanted to take his father's automated signature machine out of his hands.

Changes, inheritance decisions, modification, blank slate, invention, rebirth, the literal destruction of ancestors: it can't be any other way. One Christmas evening, Henry né Berg put his plan into effect. The last mouthful in his mouth, under the pretext of being swamped with work, he got up from the table. The son then went into his childhood bedroom to prepare his tools. When he entered the room, he was surprised by its Spartan character. He no longer remembered the linoleum on the floor, the leprotic peeling of the paint on the ceiling, and the dampness of the walls close to his rope bed. Seen from another angle, the space could really have been a cabin on board a ship that could transport you far away. First, he took off his shoes. Next he folded his things, made his bed, brushed his teeth, as though accomplishing, for the last time, the last acts of a child about to say goodnight to his parents before going to bed. He then headed towards the inner staircase that connected his mother's and father's parts of the house to his bedroom. A stuffy, dark staircase, like a lunatic's padded cell. In the past, he had spent hours in this place, making shadow-puppets with his hands, his back against the metal of the handrail. Other times he would stay there, a book in his hands, feet against the wall. This was also the service staircase where the hanged man was found. Hanged by his feet. At least this is how it appeared to the son at first, with his head upside down, in order to see the dead man right side up. A servant, no doubt. What manner of crime was this? A crime against which crime? Who the criminal? And who was "criming" thus? I don't know. The man hanging like the ham in the mountain chalet. Bag of bones. Body rigid, penis erect. The cadaver had a bent, even twisted, appearance, like two branches, one long and stretching up, the other short and reaching down, y-shaped.

The descendant descended the stairs in a terrible rage. Henry né Berg approached his father's executive door, which was double-locked. He had the key. He went in. Each of the son's movements was meticulously based on the father's. Because of this, he hesitated on the threshold. Would he walk on the strip of flooring between the wall and the weave of the rug, as his father had so many times instructed him in menacing shouts to do? Or would he advance through the middle of the canvas decorated with birds, mountains, and rivers? He began by passing through the space that separated the door from the brown leather armchair in which his father was sitting, progressing toward the middle of the rug in his bare feet. Like in those hot climates where Bedouins move around beneath tents, or like a young Filipina housekeeper in the Ambassador of France's villa, the son stood barefoot before his father. He slid as though he were on water. Stamping softly and doubly on his father's principles. The son was fixated on the cardinal pink socks sticking out from the hand-stitched Limoges moccasins before him. He stopped in front of the felt top of the secretary desk upon which the automated signature machine was enthroned. It's a strange device, in the same family as signature verifiers and stamps, which takes after the braille writing machine and the player piano. A heavy, cumbersome, and troubling instrument. In short, a ridiculous object. Henry né Berg's tense body moved towards the machine enthroned on the desk. Very suddenly, he struck and then re-struck his father's automatic signature machine with his fists. An act so violent that the large, metal-tinted paper lampshade that lit up the room cracked, ripping apart the reflective surface. The son struck out with his closed fists. Then, gripping it by its sides, he grabbed the automatic signature machine and he lifted it up, like he was wielding an axe. Elbows in the air, the son dropped his two hands and his two arms behind his shoulders, the way a lumberjack lifts his axe. With all his strength, he smashed his father's automatic signature machine against the carpet. The device burst into pieces. All the trinkets, the props, the false teeth on his father's desk, all in pieces too. Between his fingers, the son held nothing more than a heap of scrap metal. The imprint of his father's signature was separated in two, dismantled, pulverized.

During his son's outburst, Henry né Berg's father hadn't said a word. He didn't react. Shaved head, eyes half-closed, he looked like a plain-clothes monk. The man stayed seated on the pivoting brown-leather Eames armchair. In fact, during the whole of his son's outburst, the father never stopped pivoting on his seat. The effect was that Henry né Berg the younger alternately had his father's face (the once-refined face of a refined man) and then a monochromatic, Soulages-style black rectangle before him. The back of the leather chair blindly watched the son. I'm not sure his father fidgeted intentionally. His hand was trembling. If one had looked at it closely, one could have seen the subtle trembles that momentarily traveled across the veined hand lying on the armrest. Thus anticipating the jerky motions of his offspring.

Henry né Berg the younger next left his father's office and headed toward his mother's room. She was there. He caught her by surprise in her nightgown. She was working on one of the family albums that she kept in secret, using one of those yellow sticks of glue. His mother, in fact, dedicated much of her time to imagining all kinds of ludicrous genealogies. She constructed implausible family photo albums. She would spend hours sticking little pieces of cardboard printed with food and clothing brand names onto a clumsily drawn family tree with the glue stick that she now held between her two fingers, facing her son. The members of her family thus found themselves adorned with commercial labels: New Man, Uncle Ben's, Bonne Maman, Marmite, etc. Many times, the son had seen his mother leafing through an album constructed entirely from images of celebrities lifted from various newspapers and magazines. She habitually showed this album to anyone who would look at it. What the visitor discovered was stupefying. Underneath a photo of the philosopher Martin Heidegger—crafty-looking in his Bavarian costume—she had written her father's name; to the right of a snapshot of a pained-looking Georges Perec in skis at Villard-de-Lans, she had inscribed the name of her brother. And in the caption of an image depicting Adrien Wettach, aka Grock, the King of Clowns, in front of a circus tent covered in snow, she had scribbled the name of her own son. Grotesque. On the tray for various trinkets, in her room, Henry né Berg knew one could find another of these specimens. Every Sunday, from various women's magazines, his mother had patiently cut out hundreds of images depicting mothers with their sons. Snapshots showing all kinds of mothers with all kinds of sons, which she had meticulously captioned with the names of all the places she had visited with *her* only son. It was unbearable. These albums were an even cruder image of Henry né Berg's mother's dementia. These creations born from her hand, meticulously put together with maniacal care, that could be found organized in volumes in her bedroom's library, were creations of the sort that can just as easily be found in contemporary art museums, duly signed by famous artists. But they were nothing in comparison to the album that she harbored in her head. This album was one that no visitor could go see. In her mind's album, almost all the generation's possible positions were, indifferently or nearly indifferently, filled by family members. In her head, she had a hellish family, in which no one was really in their place, but where no one was truly displaced. Ultimately, it had little or no effect on her complete mental confusion. Henry né Berg couldn't use force. It was his despair against her nerves. He confronted her with the oldest of tropes: the endlessly beating heart growing fat inside each of us, this sticky schmaltz in glazed red. His was a stony heart that he no longer wanted, but had been able to offer to someone before, at a time when he could make space in it for something other than a mother's love. Then he went away. Contracts, agreements, everything was ready, reread, stamped. There was nothing left to sign. The next day, Henry né Berg's father was driven out of the bank, his mother put to the curb of their mansion. While he was at it, the son arranged for the mountain chalet to be sold. Goodbye hanged man, goodbye ham!

The parents died not long after. The son refused to attend his mother's burial. All the same, he did send a pencil pusher to confirm that nothing but ash remained of this woman's burned body. Then it was the father's turn. Around his grave, wearing their Loden coats, stood the few members of the family who were still standing. Henry walked around his now-mute father's coffin. Face to face with the body, before witnesses, he declared: "I won't say anything about my father here, given that he is still alive." Then he withdrew.

That was when Henry né Berg leased a suite on the top floor of that international hotel, formerly an artist's home, set into a rock wall, containing no fewer than eleven floors, sixty windows drawn onto the façade, and covered with a slate roof, designed to look like an open book, looking out on a lake, on the surface of which, below, I could see lights flickering in the night. And then? What to do? With his plan achieved, what would the son do now? He possessed the entire fortune. He certainly owned a majority share of the bank, properties, accounts, assets, and investments of all kinds. Some claim that he shared the spoils with his sister. Yes. A requirement of the notaries. And after?

On the path, after passing an empty bench, I came across an old man. Emerging from the shadows, strapped into his green raincoat, he looked me up and down in silence. Suddenly, he addressed me in a mountain patois cross-bred with German. He kept repeating a single word that I at first didn't understand. He began and then finished each of his strange remarks with the same three well-enunciated phonemes. In the end, I understood the discontinuous German root-word he chanted repeatedly: *"Angst,"* he was saying. *"Angst. Angst,"* he repeated. Could he be Professor Baader? My cousin? No! I left this man behind and moved on.

From the youngest age, Henry né Berg entered into a fierce conflict with the dead. The son had done much to challenge paternal authority, to reject paternal wisdom, and had even in a sense committed patricide, before, later on, becoming a man exactly like his father. In the end, like everyone else, he spent his life in the shadow of this despised man, even though he had the stature, the power, and the charm to become unlike this father, who himself (as I was occasionally able to verify when he walked by without seeing me) possessed his own entirely singular charm, power, and stature. What was he missing? To become his own shadow, to ape his forebears, to return to the point of departure. There's no other way out.

Now Henry né Berg was rich and miserable. In a frozen solitude. Ice all around him. The father had preyed on the son for so long that the son became a mere shadow of the father. Towards the end of his life, the latter began to resemble the former. Like all men, the son went bald. And like his father, he was a millionaire. Having become a bald millionaire, he sent his wife, servants, and children away from his own house, as he had long ago been sent from the living room by his parents. Later, in a familiar twist to this weakness that drives men, having hunted down his ancestors, he returned to their old passions, in this case, the hunt. Nearing his end, his need for carnage became considerable. At dawn, in all weathers, he would track in the forest, following his animal instincts. There, he trod the still-damp earth, sometimes even rolling around on the ground, which nestled under his fingernails, darkening them. Then he loaded his gun and fired at a jackrabbit's lukewarm fur, the fox's coat, or a wild boar's tanned, gray hide. Bears, bright rabbits, spherical black hedgehogs, even the yeti, they all feared him. The cold morning mist, the breath of a panicked animal, and the brief cloud caused by the explosion of

gunpowder in the rifle's barrel—this moment of deto-
nation created an abbreviated version of his spirit, the
spirit of the killer he had become. Of death. Upright
in his almond-colored boots, completely covered by
a green wool coat, a deerstalker screwed onto his head,
his mouth exhaling this combination of frost, earth,
and gunpowder, beyond cause and consequence, whys
and wherefores, the ancient and the new, pure time
without content, spirit. He reveled. He stayed rooted
in the furrow until the light of day rose and illuminated the frost on the green grass. His need for silence, his taste for barrenness, drove him to leave wet,
dripping nature just at the moment that it awakened,
and he ran to take refuge in his suite behind the bay
window, from which he could leisurely contemplate
the black, immense calm of the lake.

There I was in my reverie. It was getting late. I
moved along the path that wound for several meters
through a forest of firs. For an instant, I understood
that I had living soil beneath my feet. Close up, I could
see, mixed among the tightly woven rug of the brown
pine needles, a caterpillar population that moved along
in harmonious anarchy towards a destination that was
unknown to me. There were thousands of them on the
ground. I lifted my head and saw some sort of white
cocoons suspended in the fir trees above me, gigantic
bags of cotton that contained the many larvae of

these night-spawning organisms. I took off running. Beyond the forest, the path again seemed blue-ish. My steps now sank into the snow. The moon whitely illuminated the mountainside. White on white, which took on the cast of frost, muffled and translucent. Ice stars sparkled in the dusk light. I moved on. My friend's chalet was very far away. Sometimes, pins and needles rippled through my calves. My fingers looked like little gashes, miniscule crevasses that could only get worse. I wasn't close to death yet. A man doesn't become moribund over the course of a simple walk. I had saved all kinds of breadcrumbs in my pockets, along with nuts and dried meats. If not enough for a feast, it was at least sufficient for survival. Scraps from these men and women into whose homes I had been welcomed, accommodated, fed, and who, at the height of their pain and madness, had brought me some peace. All the same, I felt a waste of origins. The house stretched out behind me, as it did before me. In a certain sense, I was never at home. Now I knew myself to be definitively outside of the house. So much the better. A living man could nevertheless emerge from even the strongest destruction. In this spot, I had an amorous thought for Hannah née Bloch's daughter, the life at work within the body of the young woman, the high breasts shaped like two green fruits, the three summits of her cleft sex; I saw her crossing a porcelain leg over the other while taking off her bloody ballerina flats. I had fixed on the distant window like a guiding star until the moment when it disappeared from my sight, its light having been extinguished. The house had definitively vanished into the darkness. In that moment, from my feet to my head, I felt a needle-like cold penetrate me deliciously, bracingly, decisively. Then, coming around the bend, beneath the moon, I saw that extraordinary rock face.

MICHAL AJVAZ, *The Golden Age,*
The Other City.

PIERRE ALBERT-BIROT, *Grabinoulor.*

YUZ ALESHKOVSKY, *Kangaroo.*

FELIPE ALFAU, *Chromos,*
Locos.

IVAN ÂNGELO, *The Celebration,*
The Tower of Glass.

ANTÓNIO LOBO ANTUNES,
Knowledge of Hell,
The Splendor of Portugal.

ALAIN MRIAS-MISSON,
Theatre of Incest.

JOHN ASHBERY AND
JAMES SCHUYLER,
A Nest of Ninnies.

ROBERT ASHLEY, *Perfect Lives.*

GABRIELA AVIGUR-ROTEM,
Heatwave and Crazy Birds.

DJUNA BARNES, *Ladies Almanack,*
Ryder.

JOHN BARTH, *Letters,*
Sabbatical.

DONALD BARTHELME, *The King,*
Paradise.

SVETISLAV BASARA, *Chinese Letter.*

MIQUEL BAUÇÀ, *The Siege in the Room.*

RENÉ BELLETTO, *Dying.*

MAREK BIEŃCZYK, *Transparency.*

ANDREI BITOV, *Pushkin House.*

ANDREJ BLATNIK, *You Do Understand.*

LOUIS PAUL BOON, *Chapel Road,*
My Little War,
Summer in Termuren.

ROGER BOYLAN, *Killoyle.*

IGNÁCIO DE LOYOLA BRANDÃO,
Anonymous Celebrity,
Zero.

BONNIE BREMSER,
Troia: Mexican Memoirs.

CHRISTINE BROOKE-ROSE,
Amalgamemnon.

BRIGID BROPHY, *In Transit.*

GERALD L. BRUNS,
Modern Poetry and the Idea of Language.

GABRIELLE BURTON, *Heartbreak*
Hotel.

MICHEL BUTOR, *Degrees,*
Mobile.

G. CABRERA INFANTE,
Infante's Inferno,
Three Trapped Tigers.

JULIETA CAMPMPOS,
The Fear of Losing Eurydice.

ANNE CARSON, *Eros the Bittersweet.*

ORLY CASTEL-BLOOM, *Dolly City.*

LOUIS-FERDINAND CÉLINE,
Castle to Castle,
Conversations with Professor Y,
London Bridge,
Normance,
North,
Rigadoon.

MARIE CHAIX,
The Laurels of Lake Constance.

HUGO CHARTERIS, *The Tide Is Right.*

ERIC CHEVILLARD, *Demolishing*
Nisard.

MARC CHOLODENKO, *Mordechai*
Schamz.

JOSHUA COHEN, *Witz.*

EMILY HOLMES COLEMAN,
The Shutter of Snow.

ROBERT COOVER,
A Night at the Movies.

STANLEY CRAWFORD, *Log of the S.S,*
The Mrs Unguentine,
Some Instructions to My Wife.

RENÉ CREVEL, *Putting*
My Foot in It.

RALPH CUSACK, *Cadenza.*

NICHOLAS DELBANCO,
The Count of Concord,
Sherbrookes.

NIGEL DENNIS, *Cards of Identity.*

PETER DIMOCK,
A Short Rhetoric for Leaving the Family.

ARIEL DORFMFMAN, *Konfidenz.*

COLEMAN DOWELL, *Island People,*
Too Much Flesh and Jabez.

ARKADII DRAGOMOSHCHENKO,
Dust.

RIKKI DUCORNET,
The Complete Butcher's Tales,
The Fountains of Neptune,
The Jade Cabinet,
Phosphor in Dreamland.

WILLIAM EASTLAKE, *The Bamboo Bed,*
Castle Keep,
Lyric of the Circle Heart.

JEAN ECHENOZ, *Chopin's Move.*

STANLEY ELKIN, *A Bad Man,*
Criers and Kibitzers, Kibitzers and
Criers,
The Dick Gibson Show,
The Franchiser,
The Living End,
Mrs. Ted Bliss.

FRANÇOIS EMMMMANUEL,
Invitation to a Voyage.

SALVADOR ESPRIU,
Ariadne in the Grotesque Labyrinth.

LESLIE A. FIEDLER,
Love and Death in the American Novel.

JUAN FILLOY, *Op Oloop.*

ANDY FITCH, *Pop Poetics.*

GUSTAVE FLAUBERT,
Bouvard and Pécuchet.

KASS FLEISHER, *Talking out of School.*

FORD MADOX FORD,
The March of Literature.

JON FOSSE, *Aliss at the Fire,*
Melancholy.

MAX FRISCH, *I'm Not Stiller,*
Man in the Holocene.

CARLOS FUENTES, *Christopher*
Unborn, Distant Relations, Terra Nostra,
Where the Air Is Clear.

TAKEHIKO FUKUNAGA,
Flowers of Grass.

WILLIAM GADDIS, *J R,*
The Recognitions.

JANICE GALLOWAY, *Foreign Parts,*
The Trick Is to Keep Breathing.

WILLIAM H H. GASS,
Cartesian Sonata and Other Novellas,
Finding a Form,
A Temple of Texts,
The Tunnel,
Willie Masters' Lonesome Wife.

GÉRARD GAVARRY, *Hoppla! 1 2 3.*

ETIENNE GILSON,
The Arts of the Beautiful, Forms
and Substances in the Arts.

C. S S. GISCOMBE,
  Giscome Road, Here.

DOUGLAS GLOVER,
  Bad News of the Heart.

WITOLD GOMBROWICZ,
  A Kind of Testament.

PAULO EMÍLIO SALES GOMES,
  P's Three Women.

GEORGI GOSPODINOV,
  Natural Novel.

JUAN GOYTISOLO, *Count Julian,*
  Juan the Landless,
  Makbara,
  Marks of Identity.

HENRY GREEN, *Back,*
  Blindness,
  Concluding,
  Doting,
  Nothing.

JACK GREEN, *Fire the Bastards!*

JIŘÍ GRUŠA, *The Questionnaire.*

MELA HARTWIG,
  Am I a Redundant Human Being?

JOHN HAWKES, *The Passion Artist,*
  Whistlejacket.

ELIZABETH HEIGHWAY, ED.,
  Contemporary Georgian Fiction.

ALEKSANDAR HEMON, ED.,
  Best European Fiction.

AIDAN HIGGINS, *Balcony of Europe,*
  Blind Man's Bluff,
  Bornholm Night-Ferry,
  Flotsam and Jetsam,
  Langrishe, Go Down,
  Scenes from a Receding Past.

KEIZO HINO, *Isle of Dreams.*

KAZUSHI HOSAKA, *Plainsong.*

ALDOUS HUXLEY, *Antic Hay,*
  Crome Yellow,
  Point Counter Point,
  Those Barren Leaves,
  Time Must Have a Stop.

NAOYUKI II, *The Shadow of a Blue Cat.*

GERT JONKE, *The Distant Sound,*
  Geometric Regional Novel,
  Homage to Czerny,
  The System of Vienna.

JACQUES JOUET, *Mountain R,*
  Savage,
  Upstaged.

MIEKO KANAI, *The Word Book.*

YORAM KANIUK, *Life on Sandpaper.*

HUGH KENNER, Flaubert,
  Joyce and Beckett: The Stoic Comedians,
  Joyce's Voices.

DANILO KISˇ, *The Attic,*
  Garden, Ashes,
  The Lute and the Scars,
  Psalm 44,
  A Tomb for Boris Davidovich.

ANITA KONKKA, *A Fool's Paradise.*

GEORGE KONRÁD, *The City Builder.*

TADEUSZ KONWICKI,
  A Minor Apocalypse,
  The Polish Complex.

MENIS KOUMANDAREAS, *Koula.*

ELAINE KRAF,
  The Princess of 72nd Street.

JIM KRUSOE, *Iceland.*

AYŞE KULIN,
  Farewell: A Mansion in Occupied Istanbul.

CHRISTINE MONTALBETTI,
The Origin of Man,
Western.

WARREN MOTTE, *Fables of the Novel:*
French Fiction since 1990,
Fiction Now: The French Novel in the 21st
Century,
Oulipo: A Primer of Potential Literature.

GERALD MURNANE,
Barley Patch, Inland.

YVES NAVARRE,
Our Share of Time,
Sweet Tooth.

DOROTHY NELSON, *In Night's City,*
Tar and Feathers.

ESHKOL NEVO, *Homesick.*

WILFRIDO D D. NOLLEDO,
But for the Lovers.

FLANN O'BRIEN, *At Swim-Two-Birds,*
The Best of Myles,
The Dalkey Archive,
The Hard Life,
The Poor Mouth,
The Third Policeman.

CLAUDE OLLIER, *The Mise-en-Scène,*
Wert and the Life Without End.

GIOVANNI ORELLI, *Walaschek's Dream.*

PATRIK OUŘEDNÍK, *Europeana,*
The Opportune Moment, 1855.

BORIS PAHOR, *Necropolis.*

FERNANDO DEL PASO,
News from the Empire,
Palinuro of Mexico.

ROBERT PINGET, *The Inquisitory,*
Mahu or The Material,
Trio.

MANUEL PUIG,
Betrayed by Rita Hayworth,
The Buenos Aires Affair,
Heartbreak Tango.

RAYMYMOND QUENEAU,
The Last Days, Odile,
Pierrot Mon Ami,
Saint Glinglin.

ANN QUIN, *Berg,*
Passages,
Three,
Tripticks.

ISHMAEL REED,
The Free-Lance Pallbearers,
The Last Days of Louisiana Red,
Ishmael Reed: The Plays,
Juice!,
Reckless Eyeballing,
The Terrible Threes,
The Terrible Twos,
Yellow Back Radio Broke-Down.

JASIA REICHARDT,
15 Journeys Warsaw to London.

NOËLLE REVAZ,
With the Animals.

JOÃO UBALDO RIBEIRO,
House of the Fortunate Buddhas.

JEAN RICARDOU, *Place Names.*

RAINER MARIA RILKE,
The Notebooks of Malte Laurids Brigge.

JULIÁN RÍOS, *The House of Ulysses,*
Larva: A Midsummer Night's Babel,
Poundemonium,
Procession of Shadows.

AUGUSTO ROA BASTOS, *I the*
Supreme.

DANIËL ROBBERECHTS,
Arriving in Avignon.

JEAN ROLIN,
  The Explosion of the Radiator Hose.

OLIVIER ROLIN, *Hotel Crystal.*

ALIX CLEO ROUBAUD, *Alix's Journal.*

JACQUES ROUBAUD,
  The Form of a City Changes Faster, Alas,
  Than the Human Heart,
  The Great Fire of London,
  Hortense in Exile,
  Hortense Is Abducted,
  The Loop,
  Mathematics, The Plurality of Worlds of
  Lewis, The Princess Hoppy,
  Some Thing Black.

RAYMYMOND ROUSSEL,
  Impressions of Africa.

VEDRANA RUDAN, *Night.*

STIG SÆTERBAKKEN, *Siamese,*
  Self Control.

LYDIE SALVAYRE,
  The Company of Ghosts,
  The Lecture,
  The Power of Flies.

LUIS RAFAEL SÁNCHEZ,
  Macho Camacho's Beat.

SEVERO SARDUY, *Cobra & Maitreya.*

NATHALIE SARRAUTE,
  Do You Hear Them?,
  Martereau,
  The Planetarium.

ARNO SCHMIDT, *Collected Novellas,*
  Collected Stories,
  Nobodaddy's Children,
  Two Novels.

ASAF SCHURR, *Motti.*

GAIL SCOTT, *My Paris.*

DAMION SEARLS, *What We Were Doing*
  and Where We Were Going.

JUNE AKERS SEESE,
  Is This What Other Women Feel Too?,
  What Waiting Really Means.

BERNARD SHARE, *Inish, Transit.*

VIKTOR SHKLOVSKY, *Bowstring,*
  Knight's Move,
  A Sentimental Journey: Memoirs
  1917–1922,
  Energy of Delusion: A Book on Plot,
  Literature and Cinematography,
  Theory of Prose,
  Third Factory,
  Zoo, or Letters Not about Love.

PIERRE SINIAC, *The Collaborators.*

KJERSTI A. SKOMSVOLD,
  The Faster I Walk, the Smaller I Am.

JOSEF ŠKVORECKÝ,
  The Engineer of Human Souls.

GILBERT SORRENTINO,
  Aberration of Starlight,
  Blue Pastoral,
  Crystal Vision,
  Imaginative Qualities of Actual Things,
  Mulligan Stew,
  Pack of Lies,
  Red the Fiend,
  The Sky Changes,
  Something Said,
  Splendide-Hôtel,
  Steelwork,
  Under the Shadow.

W. M. SPACKMAN, *The Complete*
  Fiction.

ANDRZEJ STASIUK, *Dukla,*
  Fado.

FOR A FULL LIST OF PUBLICATIONS, VISIT: www.dalkeyarchive.com

⬜ SELECTED DALKEY ARCHIVE TITLES

GERTRUDE STEIN, *The Making of Americans, A Novel of Thank You.*

LARS SVENDSEN, *A Philosophy of Evil.*

PIOTR SZEWC, *Annihilation.*

GONÇALO M. TAVARES, *Jerusalem, Joseph Walser's Machine, Learning to Pray in the Age of Technique.*

LUCIAN DAN TEODOROVICI, *Our Circus Presents . . .*

NIKANOR TERATOLOGEN, *Assisted Living.*

STEFAN THEMERSON, *Hobson's Island, The Mystery of the Sardine, Tom Harris.*

TAEKO TOMIOKA, *Building Waves.*

JOHN TOOMEY, *Sleepwalker.*

JEAN-PHILIPPPPPE TOUSSAINT, *The Bathroom, Camera, Monsieur, Reticence, Running Away, Self-Portrait Abroad, Television, The Truth about Marie.*

DUMITRU TSEPENEAG, *Hotel Europa, The Necessary Marriage, Pigeon Post, Vain Art of the Fugue.*

ESTHER TUSQUETS, *Stranded.*

DUBRAVKA UGRESIC, *Lend Me Your Character, Thank You for Not Reading.*

TOR ULVEN, *Replacement.*

MATI UNT, *Brecht at Night, Diary of a Blood Donor, Things in the Night.*

ÁLVARO URIBE AND OLIVIA SEARS, EDS., *Best of Contemporary Mexican Fiction.*

ELOY URROZ, *Friction, The Obstacles.*

LUISA VALENZUELA, *Dark Desires and the Others, He Who Searches.*

PAUL VERHAEGHEN, *Omega Minor.*

AGLAJA VETERANYI, *Why the Child Is Cooking in the Polenta.*

BORIS VIAN, *Heartsnatcher.*

LLORENÇ VILLALONGA, *The Dolls' Room.*

TOOMAS VINT, *An Unending Landscape.*

ORNELA VORPSI, *The Country Where No One Ever Dies.*

AUSTRYN WAINHOUSE, *Hedyphagetica.*

CURTIS WHITE, *America's Magic Mountain, The Idea of Home, Memories of My Father Watching TV, Requiem.*

DIANE WILLIAMS, *Excitability: Selected Stories, Romancer Erector.*

DOUGLAS WOOLF, *Wall to Wall, Ya! & John-Juan.*

FOR A FULL LIST OF PUBLICATIONS, VISIT: www.dalkeyarchive.com

.